# The Little Prince

## A VISUAL DICTIONARY

CHRISTOPHE QUILLIEN

CERNUNNOS

15-27, rue Moussorgski
75018 Paris

www.cernunnospublishing.com

 www.facebook.com/Cernunnos

First published in 2016 by CERNUNNOS
An imprint of Mediatoon Licensing

The Little Prince®
© Antoine de Saint-Exupery Estate 2016

Director of publication: Rodolphe Lachat
Cernunnos logo design: Mark Ryden
Graphic Design: Elisabeth Hébert
Layout: Cerise Heurteur
Translation from French: Passport
English Language Services, based in
part on the Katherine Woods editions.

ISBN: 978-2-37495-012-9
Copyright registration: October 2016

2016 2017 2018 2019 2020 /
10 9 8 7 6 5 4 3 2 1
Printed in Italy by Stige.

**Acknowledgments**

With thanks to Rodolphe Lachat,
the eternal little prince (and occasional
businessman) on planet Huginn;
to Sabrina Lamotte, Rue Moussorgski's
very own rose; and to Philippe Vallotti,
the sleek fox responsible for taming
the text to match the illustrations
and for playing the railway switchman
with his vigilant reading and rereading.
Thanks also go to the whole team
at the Saint-Exupéry estate for their
support and invaluable assistance:
Olivier d'Agay, Morgane Fontan,
Thomas Rivière, and Virgil Tanase.
Finally, well done to Elisabeth Hébert
and Cerise Heurteur for having drawn,
not a little sheep, but this beautifully
presented book.

Cernunnos publishing wishes to extend
special thanks to Philippe Vallotti for his
admirable contribution to this project,
worthy of his unconditional love for
*The Little Prince*.

# The Little Prince

## A VISUAL DICTIONARY

CHRISTOPHE QUILLIEN

CERNUNNOS

# Contents

Antoine Saint-Exupéry:
Biographical Timeline 6
Foreword 9

## 1. Antoine de Saint-Exupéry 11

A Happy Childhood 12

His Calling in the Air 14

First Letters, First Writings 16

Saint-Exupéry, Artist 18

Adventures
with Aéropostale 20

Saint-Exupéry, Writer 22

Saint-Exupéry and Women 24

Exile in America 26

The Final Mission 28

## 2. The Origins of The Little Prince 31

Biographical and
Personal Sources 32

The Little Prince,
an Editor's Request 35

Léon Werth,
the "Best Friend" 36

Sketches of
the Little Prince 38

The Manuscript and
Proof Sets 40

## 3. The Little Prince, the Oeuvre 43

First Editions 45

French and
French-language Editions 46

An Unpublished Chapter 48

Variations of the Text 50

The Little Prince on
Earth: Translations 56

The Little Prince on
Earth: Illustrations 58

Critical Reception 62

## 4. The Little Prince Universe 65

The Aviator 66

The Little Prince 68

The Fox 70

The Snake 71

The Turkish Astronomer 73

The King 74

The Conceited Man 74

The Drunkard 75

The Businessman 75

The Lamplighter 76

The Geographer 76

The Desert Flower 77

The Echo 77

The Roses 78

The Railway Switchman 78

The Hunter 79

The Merchant 79

The Little Prince
Environment:

The Earth 80

The Desert 81

The Star 81

Asteroid B 612 82

The Baobabs 83

Objects 84

## The Little Prince Quotations 88

## 5. The Little Prince Bookshelf 91

Lettres à l'inconnue 92

Sequels and Imitations 94

The Little Prince
Archive 96

Books on the
Animated Series 100

## The Little Prince: Testimonials 102

## 6. The Little Prince On Screen 105

Cinema 106

Television 114

## 7. The Little Prince On Stage — 123

Theater — 124

Opera and Musical Productions — 128

Multimedia Shows — 132

Audio Recordings — 134

## 8. The Little Prince in Comics and Youth Literature — 139

*Saint-Exupéry, the Final Flight* — 140

Joann Sfar's *The Little Prince* — 142

The Little Prince: New Adventures — 144

Comic Book Tributes — 150

*The Pilot and the Little Prince* — 154

## 9. Inspired By The Little Prince — 157

Merchandise — 158

Learning with The Little Prince — 164

Jean-Charles de Castelbajac, Prince of Fashion — 168

The Little Prince in Advertising — 172

## 10. The Little Prince Around the World — 175

The Little Prince Theme Park — 176

And Elsewhere? — 180

## 11. The Little Prince and Us — 187

Everyone Loves The Little Prince! — 188

Collectors — 196

The Little Prince and Society — 198

Exhibitions — 200

Non-Profit Organizations — 202

Conclusion — 204

## Bibliography — 206
## Image Credits — 207

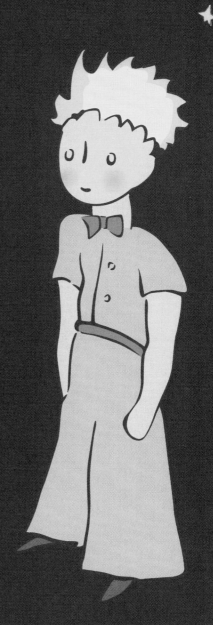

# Antoine de Saint-Exupéry: Biographical Timeline

**1900** — Antoine Jean-Baptiste Marie Roger Pierre de Saint-Exupéry is born in Lyon.

**1904** — Jean de Saint-Exupéry, his father, dies.

**1912** — Takes his maiden flight.

**1917** — His brother François dies.

**1919** — Fails the oral exam at the Naval Academy. Enters the École des Beaux-Arts in Paris to study architecture.

Discovers the Parisian literary scene, meets the team of the literary journal *Nouvelle Revue Française* (NRF).

**1921** — Completes his national service in the French 2nd Aerial Fighter Regiment in Strasbourg. Has his first flying lessons and is involved in his first plane crash.

**1922** — Becomes a pilot for the fighter wing in the French 34th Air Regiment.

**1923** — Becomes engaged to Louise de Vilmorin but it is broken off.

Leaves the Air Force.

Becomes an accountant in Paris.

**1924- 1925** — Works as a sales representative in Greater Paris, selling trucks.

**1926** — Publishes his first short story *The Aviator* in the literary review *Le Navire d'argent*.

His oldest sister Marie-Madeleine dies.

Begins flying for the Latécoère Group based in Toulouse, where he meets Jean Mermoz and Henri Guillaumet.

**1927** — Works as an air mail pilot for Toulouse–Casablanca and Dakar–Casablanca routes.

Posted in Cape Juby, south of Morocco, for 18 months, where he writes *Southern Mail* (1929).

**1929** — Works as the director of air mail company Aeroposta Argentina in Buenos Aires.

**1930** — Named *Chevalier* in the French Legion of Honor for his service to civil aeronautics.

Meets Consuelo Gómez Carrillo, née Suncín-Sandoval.

Writes *Night Flight*.

**1931** — Marries Consuelo in Agay (Var).

Works as a night pilot between Casablanca and Port-Étienne.

*Night Flight* is published (with a preface by André Gide) and wins the Prix Femina.

**1932** — Publishes articles in *Marianne*, a weekly literary magazine published by Gallimard.

**1933** — Works as a seaplane test pilot.

Screenwriter for Raymond Bernard's film *Anne-Marie*.

**1934** — Joins the advertising department for the newly created Air France.

Works on the screenplay for *Southern Mail*.

*Night Flight*, the film adapted from his book, is released.

**1935** — Reports from Moscow for the daily newspaper *Paris-Soir*.

Meets Léon Werth.

Crashes his plane during the Paris to Saigon air race.

**1936** — Begins work writing *The Wisdom of the Sands*.

Reports on the Spanish Civil War for the daily newspaper *L'Intransigeant*.

Jean Mermoz disappears over the South Atlantic. Saint-Exupéry devotes several radio and press reports to him.

**1937** — Reports on the Spanish Civil War for newspapers *L'Intransigeant* and *Paris-Soir*.

Files several aeronautics patents.

**1938** — Maintains air routes between Casablanca–Timbuktu and Dakar–Casablanca.

Crashes his plane in Guatemala City during the New York to Tierra del Fuego (Argentina) air race.

Writes *Wind, Sand and Stars*.

Files several aeronautics patents.

**1939** — Publishes *Wind, Sand and Stars*, which earns the Grand Prix du roman from the Académie française and selected Book of the Month and winner of the National Book Award in the US.

Promoted to *Officier* in the French Legion of Honor.

Mobilized on September 4 and assigned to technical training. Transfers to the 2/33 reconnaissance squadron based in Orconte (Marne).

**1940** — Flies reconnaissance missions over Arras, inspiring *Flight to Arras*.

Inducted into the Order of the Air Force, decorated with the War Cross. Demobilized following the armistice between France and Germany, he continues writing *The Wisdom of the Sands*.

Henri Guillaumet dies.

Leaves for New York with filmmaker Jean Renoir.

**1941** — Undergoes an operation in Los Angeles.

During his convalescence, writes *Flight to Arras*.

Rereads *The Little Mermaid* with French actress Annabella.

**1942** — His wife Consuelo arrives in New York.

*Flight to Arras* is published in English in the US, illustrated by his friend Bernard Lamotte.

Gives conferences in Canada.

Begins work on *The Little Prince*.

*Flight to Arras* is published in France (as *Pilote de Guerre*) but is subsequently banned at the request of the governing German authorities.

On American radio on November 22, Saint-Exupéry calls for all French citizens overseas to unite. On November 29, *The New York Times Magazine* reprints his appeal under the title *An Open Letter to Frenchmen Everywhere*.

**1943** — Publishes *Letter to a Hostage*.

Publishes *The Little Prince* on April 6 with publishing house Reynal & Hitchcock.

Joins the 2/33 squadron, flies his first reconnaissance mission over French territory in June.

Banned from flying in July following a crash landing while returning from a photography mission.

Devotes himself to writing *The Wisdom of the Sands* and studying mathematics.

Promoted to Commandant, his flight status is restored and he rejoins the squadron.

**1944** — Saint-Exupéry takes off on his final reconnaissance mission over the region between Grenoble and Annecy on July 31, 8:35 AM; reported missing at 2:30 PM.

**1998** — His identity chain bracelet is discovered off the coast of Marseille.

**2004** — French authorities confirm that found wreckage is from his lost aircraft.

**2008** — German pilot Horst Rippert claims recalling shooting down Saint-Exupéry (to this day, no evidence has been found to support his claim).

"I should have liked to begin
this story in the fashion
            of fairy tales.
I should have liked to say:
    'Once upon a time there was
            a little prince who lived
on a planet that was scarcely
                any bigger than himself,
and who had need of a friend...'"

# Foreword

This book tells the story of a young boy like no other. He is called the little prince. We do not know his age, nor even where he comes from (where is the asteroid B 612, exactly?), nor have we the faintest idea whether he will return to Earth one day. We don't even know where he was born. "Easy!" slightly over-grounded grown-ups will tell you, "He was born in the USA in 1943, in a book written by Antoine de Saint-Exupéry." These grown-ups have answers to everything, just not very imaginative ones. What do they know? Perhaps the little prince was born in the desert in Morocco, or in the tales that Madame de Saint-Exupéry used to read to her son, or in the drawings that Antoine would scribble everywhere he went. Or, perhaps simply in the young Antoine's amazement for the fairy tales he found to be "life's only truth".

It also tells the story of Saint-Exupéry. Or rather, of Saint-Exupéries: child, accountant, aviator, writer, inventor, philosopher, and lover of women. By the time he was 10 years old, his future was already mapped out. He wrote, drew, and dreamed of flying planes. He built a flying machine that could never leave the ground, and that would serve as the first in a long string of accidents. Already "Saint-Ex'" was piercing through Antoine. With the youth's curiosity and questioning, the character of the little prince was never all that far from his own. In his melancholy, too, there is a strong resemblance between character and creator.

Saint-Exupéry once wrote that he was "made to be a gardener". Life, however, had other plans, and so much the better. For, through his books, he gave us something to dream about: a feat just as important as gardening. To read *Wind, Sand and Stars* and *Night Flight* is to soar over the desert by the light of the moon, experiencing a silence broken only by the wind as it caresses the plane's cockpit. To read *The Little Prince* is to open the door to a wondrous world whose richness never runs out, to which we can return no matter how old we grow; and still, every time, discover new answers to old questions—as well as being struck with new ones. How could we ever see sunsets, streetlamps, and baobabs the same way again?

This encyclopedia sets out to explore the universe of *The Little Prince* and its hero in all of its many forms. There are so many different occasions that one might have him, or some sort of incarnation of his, along for part of the journey. For the little prince is forever being reborn and reinvented: on screen and stage; in opera and books (some have even imagined sequels to Saint-Exupéry's tale); in language learning guides and comic books; in song and fashion; in musical productions and commercials; in highway service stations and cartoons; and even on bank notes (ironic, given that Saint-Exupéry never kept bank notes for long: money burned holes in his pockets). These new and updated icons sometimes take certain liberties, "inspired by" the original, when compared to the hallowed formula. And occasionally, a reworking seems to lack any inspiration whatsoever, but such is undoubtedly the price to pay for his celebrity.

The little prince is everywhere: alongside patients at the Pequeño Principe hospital in Brazil; with young victims of Hurricane Mitch in Honduras; helping sick children's dreams come true, thanks to the organizations bearing his name. Orson Welles dreamed of adapting the story to film; James Dean saw himself in him. But no need to be famous or to venture into the Sahara where he first appeared to know that he is here beside us. It is enough to know how to look, even if the essential is invisible to the eye. Most importantly, it is enough to know how to feel.

*The Little Prince* has been translated into 270 languages. The character created by Antoine de Saint-Exupéry is universal. The little prince laughs at the borders and barriers that divide men. He has neither papers, nor nationality, nor religion. And why would he need them? *The Little Prince* belongs to everyone.

1- Antoine de Saint-Exupéry

# A Happy Childhood

up the most imaginative games, he made everyone else follow him, and he never took "no" for an answer. Antoine was intrepid, a headstrong daredevil, and rarely obedient. His unruly predisposition was only encouraged by his governesses, who were far too indulgent to assert any authority over him.

*"GROWING UP WAS A MISTAKE. REALLY. I WAS SO HAPPY IN MY CHILDHOOD."*

Antoine de Saint-Exupéry was born in Lyon on June 29, 1900 in a bedroom of the family apartment; the third of five children. On vacations, the family would take up residence in their château at Saint-Maurice-de-Rémens in the Bugey region. The 18th-century building belonged to Gabrielle de Lestrange, the great-aunt and godmother of Antoine's mother. It was at this manor house, surrounded by acres of parkland disposed to all sorts of adventures, that the young Antoine would lead his sisters Marie-Madeleine (Biche), Simone, and Gabrielle (Didi), his brother François, and their cousins into his games.

The children thronged the maze of "luminous, warm rooms" in the château. Antoine was captivated by the sitting room where "grown-ups" would play bridge and strike up mysterious conversations. He was fascinated by the imposing bookshelf in the billiards room. At night, comforting shadows cast by the wood stove would soothe Antoine in his sometimes-fitful sleep. His brothers and sisters nicknamed him "The Sun King": he liked being in charge; he made

PREVIOUS Antoine (standing), his brother François, and their mother Marie de Saint-Exupéry, 1905.

TOP LEFT Antoine's mother, Marie de Saint-Exupéry (née Fonscolombe).

ABOVE The Saint-Exupéry children: Marie-Madeleine, Gabrielle, François, Antoine, and Simone.

RIGHT Jean de Saint-Exupéry, Antoine's father.

*"I HAVE LIVED A GREAT DEAL AMONG GROWN-UPS. I HAVE SEEN THEM CLOSE AT HAND. AND THAT HASN'T MUCH IMPROVED MY OPINION OF THEM."*

SAINT-MAURICE DE RÉMENS (Ain)

When he wasn't climbing the furniture, Antoine was sliding down the endless corridors after having flung himself from the banisters. He would lose himself in the grounds that he crisscrossed on foot or on bicycle. In his moments of calm, he would write short plays for his brother and sisters to act out.

Antoine was nine when his family moved to Le Mans. He was educated by Jesuits and proved to be a talented but temperamental young boy. He preferred his poetry to his schoolwork. More often than not, his professors would catch him daydreaming rather than focusing on his workbooks. But if he earned the nickname "Moon Spike" among his classmates, it wasn't for any romantic sonnets inspired by the Earth's satellite, but for his charming upturned nose… His childhood was not, however, free of trauma. He was only four years old when his father suffered a fatal stroke on a railway station platform. In 1917, his brother François died in his arms from a bout of rheumatic fever, bequeathing him, as Antoine described years later in *Flight over Arras*, "a steam engine, a bicycle, and a rifle." François was fourteen years old. For Antoine, it marked the end of his childhood and a certain insouciance.

**TOP** Antoine and his aunt at the Château de Mole in the Var department, 1906.

**ABOVE** The château at Saint-Maurice-de-Rémens in the Ain department.

**LEFT** From the age of seven onwards, Saint-Exupéry kept his "treasures", his letters, and his photographs in a chest. "This chest is the only thing of value in my life," he wrote to his friend Rinette.

13

# His Calling in the Air

Antoine dreamed of flying like a bird. Before he was even ten years old, he imagined a sort of flying machine, which he cobbled together with the help of a local village carpenter. It was a "sail bicycle", equipped with a wooden framework attached to the handlebars, over which hung a flag. The experiment came to an abrupt end; the vehicle ended its trajectory in a ditch without ever having left the ground... Despite his skinned knees, Antoine didn't give up. Two years later, exploring the region on his bike, he discovered a small airfield in Ambérieu, six kilometers from the château. He managed to convince

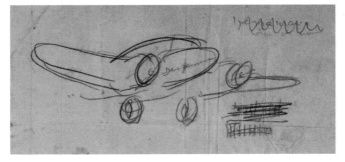

*"SO THEN I CHOSE
ANOTHER PROFESSION,
AND LEARNED
TO PILOT AIRPLANES."*

a certain Gabriel Wroblewski-Salvez, pilot and brother of an aircraft designer, to take him on his first flight, insisting (untruthfully) that his mother harbored no objection to the arrangement. After twice circling over the grounds, Antoine was happy: he had finally made his dream come true. The disciplinary slap he received from his mother upon returning home was a minor detail. At 12 years old, he had found his calling.

When the time came for military service in 1921, Antoine de Saint-Exupéry obviously chose the Air Force. But before he could be admitted as a pilot, he would need to obtain his civilian pilot's license. He started at the 2nd Aerial Fighter Regiment in Neuhof (near Strasbourg) as a "crawler": working on the ground maintaining aircraft and the runway. Meanwhile, he was chomping at the bit, taking private flying lessons, paid for by his mother, in a Farman 40. After two weeks of theory and logging a mere two and a half hours with an instructor, he took off for his first solo flight in a Sopwith. At that time, aviation was still a dangerous exploit, an extreme sport practiced by daredevils and eccentrics. Indeed, two years after Antoine's maiden flight, the Wroblewski-Salvez brothers perished flying one of their creations. Aviators were the heroes of their times.

From his first sorties, Antoine developed his own way of flying planes: a mix of carelessness, a conscious lack of discipline, amateurism, and a refusal to take advice. The list of his "acts of valor" is interminable. He misplaced his goggles; lost control of his aircraft during takeoff; blew an objective for want of a pencil; dropped bombs—dummies, thankfully—on the wrong locations... Thus, he earned a fair reputation for being a plane-wrecker that would follow him throughout his whole life. Nevertheless, in 1921, he received his military flying certification in Casablanca, Morocco, where he had been transferred to the 37th Aerial Fighter Regiment. In October 1922, he was appointed Sub-lieutenant in the reserve and reposted to the 34th Air Regiment at Le Bourget. This time, his flying career had finally taken wing.

**OPPOSITE, TOP** Antoine de Saint-Exupéry aboard his Caudron Simoun, 1935.

**OPPOSITE, BOTTOM LEFT** Sketch of an airplane by Saint-Exupéry.

**OPPOSITE, BOTTOM RIGHT** One of the patents registered by the writer-aviator-inventor.

**TOP** Saint-Exupéry standing beside his plane, registered F-ANRY (after the first two letters of his first name and the last two letters of his surname).

**LEFT** The dispirited aviator gazes at his Caudron Simoun after crashing in the Libyan desert during the Paris to Saigon air race.

15

# First Letters, First Writings

When he imagined his future, the little Antoine saw himself more as an architect than as a writer. But the written word fascinated him. "When I was four and a half, I burned with the desire to read a real book," he wrote in his essay *Books I Remember*. Throughout his childhood, his mother would tell him stories and read him Hans Christian Anderson's fairy tales. He felt an irresistible pull toward books, those peculiar objects covered in strange runes that he could not yet decipher. His appetite for reading came early in life and soon branched into writing. He would loot volumes from the family library at the château in Saint-Maurice, which would litter the floor of his bedroom. He loved their colored covers, their full-page illustrations, and the enchanting smell of the paper.

---

**RIGHT** In his letters, Antoine united his passion for writing and his talent for drawing.

**OPPOSITE, CENTER** Antoine's first-person tale of a top hat for a "French narrative" composition in 1914.

**OPPOSITE** Antoine's brother and sisters prepare to perform one of his plays.

*"I LIVED IN PERFECT TRANQUILITY, WAITING FOR THE DAY WHEN I WOULD MAKE MY DEBUT ON THE WORLD'S STAGE."*

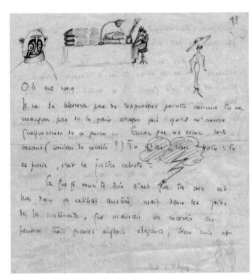

As soon as he could write, Antoine would pen short plays that he would perform for adults. Early on, he also developed a habit that he would never cease: writing letters to his mother, which bear testament to the intense love he felt for her. At age thirteen, he started up a little paper with his classmates, putting himself in charge of the poetry section; far from attracting the admiration of his teachers, who shared little enthusiasm for his budding literary "talents", it only earned him hours of detention. It should be said that the copious spelling mistakes that littered his texts hardly could have helped his case... No matter; he was writing, and that's all that mattered to Antoine. When he was fourteen years

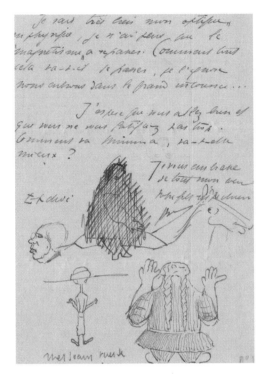

old, he wrote an essay imagining an odyssey made by a top hat. The style was alert, the tone upbeat. "I was born in a large hat factory. For several days, I endured all sorts of torture: they cut me up, stretched me, varnished me. Finally, one evening, I was sent with my brothers to the largest hat milliner in Paris. Placed in the shop window, I was one of the finest riding top hats: so glossy that ladies passing by couldn't help but admire their reflections in my shining patent leather; so elegant that no distinguished gentleman saw me who didn't wish to own me. I lived in perfect tranquility, waiting for the day when I would make my debut on the world's stage."

A year later, Antoine discovered literature's great classics. He read Balzac, Baudelaire, and Dostoevsky. He wrote poems and a libretto for an operetta. And yet, these budding literary activities could not save him from poor marks at school that more often than not relegated him to the bottom of the class. But throughout his life, writing remained an effective remedy against his anxieties and a companion in his solitude.

# Saint-Exupéry, Artist

Once an adult, he continued his drawing, unlike the majority of people who cease the practice (as drawing is not deemed a particularly serious activity and is therefore perceived as incompatible with their recently achieved status of "grown-up"). He sketched his friends during his military service in Casablanca. Between 1925 and 1926, he would doodle humorous, self-deprecating little scenes on the letterhead of the restaurants and hotels he visited.

*"GROWN-UPS' ADVICE WAS TO LAY ASIDE MY DRAWINGS OF BOA CONSTRICTORS, WHETHER FROM THE INSIDE OR THE OUTSIDE."*

The earliest saved copies of Antoine de Saint-Exupéry's graphic works date from his childhood years, around 1911. They consist of doodles sketched in the margins of letters, of poems written in calligraphy and illustrated in pencil or watercolor. Antoine dreamed up witty skits for his mother, sisters, and friends. He liberally caricatured the recipients of his letters (which, we imagine, may not always have been appreciated). But he was never satisfied with the results, as evidenced by the written remarks accompanying his illustrations: "My drawings are so horrible," he wrote in a letter from 1918. "I can't draw... drat!" he lamented the following year. Or, "I am forced to accept this drawing for the simple reason that my lack of skill prevents me at the outset from imagining what the end result will be."

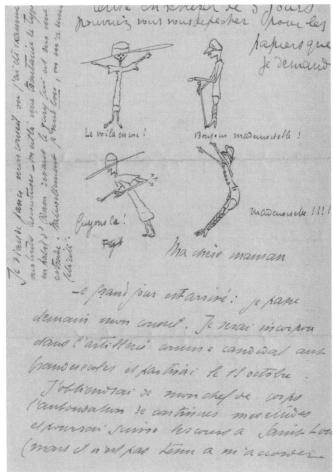

**ABOVE LEFT** Portrait of his friend, the painter Bernard Lamotte (1942-1943).

**ABOVE** Letter to his mother, adorned with caricatures of his sisters and a burlesque skit.

These scenes are testament to Saint-Exupéry's *ennui* in his new profession as a sales representative in charge of selling trucks. He would draw at any time and on anything: letters, menus, books he gave to his friends, bills, or just loose sheets of paper, that is, when he wasn't drawing directly on the table of a restaurant—one of the many surfaces to which his subtle line added a poetic dimension. His society life during the 1930s inspired numerous female portraits, a mix of the world's women: coquettes or young female nudes. His male characters possess a slight fantastic touch; they are disturbing, mysterious creatures with disproportionate faces. He also worked on self-portraits, drawings of animals, and technical drawings.

*"TODAY, I DISCOVERED WHAT I WAS MADE FOR: THE CONTÉ CHARCOAL PENCIL."*

"Today, I discovered what I was made for: the Conté charcoal pencil," he wrote to his mother. Saint-Exupéry mixed graphic techniques, principally using quill and ink, the traditional tools of a writer; but he also used graphite pencil, colored pencil, poster paint, watercolor, and ink and wash. He preferred working on onion paper. Rarely did he sign his work, freely distributing his drawings among his friends and never hesitating to throw away those that he deemed failures—which is to say, the vast majority. Antoine de Saint-Exupéry's oeuvre should not only be considered for his writing, but also his drawings, which are full of richness, poetry, and cheerful humor. From this perspective, *The Little Prince*, with its mix of text and illustrations—which, might we add, go far beyond simply illustrating the text—no doubt best expresses and presents the fullest picture of the scope of his talent.

**ABOVE LEFT** Letter sent by "Saint-Ex" to his Aéropostale colleagues after he was hospitalized in Dakar, 1927.

**ABOVE** Saint-Exupéry depicted himself in the writing process in this letter sent from Casablanca to his friend Henri Guillaumet, 1932.

**BELOW** Letter to his sister.

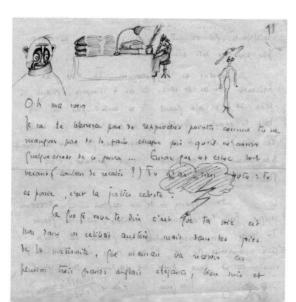

# Adventures With Aéropostale

LEFT The crew of pilots and engineers at Aéropostale.

BELOW LEFT AND BELOW (respectively) Henri Guillaumet and Jean Mermoz, colleagues and friends of Saint-Exupéry.

In 1926, Antoine de Saint-Exupéry was hired by Latécoère, a company named after its founder, an industrialist convinced that aviation had a role to play in transporting mail as well as passengers. Reporting to Didier Daurat, Antoine began work as a mechanic and was tasked with dismantling and cleaning engines. He met aviators Jean Mermoz and Henri Guillaumet and so began a long friendship between them. Antoine's first flight for Latécoère was from Toulouse to Alicante, Spain. Guillaumet proved an invaluable teacher and Saint-Exupéry benefitted from his friend's direct experience of the route. From indispensable recommendations to pilot survival tips, his lessons were not of the sort found in flying manuals. Guillaumet taught him how to get his bearings using a stream; or, say, how these three orange trees indicated a possible landing site in the middle of a field. "Little by little, the Spain of my map became a sort of fairytale

*"IN THE EXACT PLACE SHE STOOD, I MARKED THE SHEPHERDESS WHO THE GEOGRAPHERS HAD OVERLOOKED."*

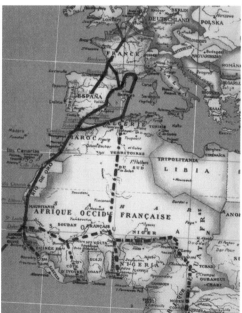

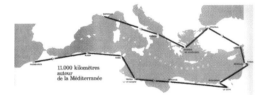

landings from engine trouble were held for ransom by Moorish tribes. For seventeen months, Antoine led a monastic life in that isolated post. The company's planes passed just once a week. He grew bored. He slept on a straw mattress on top of a plank. At night, he would work on the manuscript that would become *Southern Mail* as a means of coping with his insomnia. He learned Arabic in order to negotiate with the Moors and rescue aviators who broke down in the desert. His colleagues praised his courage, something that he would never acknowledge ("I was simply doing my job," he would say).

In the summer of 1929, the company made him director of Aeroposta Argentina in Buenos Aires. Latécoère was looking ahead, persuaded that the future of commercial aviation lay in the establishment of routes connecting Europe with the large capital cities in South America. At that point, transatlantic travel was possible thanks to new, more reliable engines. But Antoine didn't like Buenos Aires, a lonely city far away from everything, just like Cape Juby. His only comfort came from his aerial escapades, scouting new air routes for the future. In January 1931, Antoine returned to France. In his bag, he carried the manuscript for his next book, *Night Flight*.

universe under my lamp." Saint-Exupéry wrote. "I made Xs to mark refuges and traps. I marked this farmer, this brook, these thirty sheep. And, in the exact place she stood, I marked the shepherdess who the geographers had overlooked."

In 1927, after spending six months crisscrossing the Toulouse–Casablanca and Casablanca–Dakar routes, Antoine was transferred to Cape Juby on the southern border of Morocco in the Spanish Sahara. The year before, the Latécoère Group had been renamed the Compagnie générale aéropostale. Cape Juby was the station where the Aéropostale pilots could rest, and refuel their Breguet 14s. The journey was a dangerous one. Unlucky pilots forced to make emergency

**THIS PAGE** Advertising posters and maps showing Aéropostale routes.

# Saint-Exupéry, Writer

In April 1926, Antoine de Saint-Exupéry published a short story called *The Aviator* in the review *Navire d'argent*, founded by publisher and bookseller Adrienne Monnier. Jean Prévost, the journal's copyeditor, who collaborated on the *Nouvelle Revue Française* for Éditions Gallimard, had a sense of Antoine's potential. He recommended Saint-Exupéry to Gaston Gallimard, who had him sign a contract for four books. The venture could have got off to a bad start: his head in the clouds on solid ground as in the air, "Saint-Ex" first lost his manuscript before rewriting it from memory. Then, he arrived late for a meeting with Prévost, who decided not to wait for him...

**TOP RIGHT** Promotion for the release of *Flight to Arras*.

**TOP CENTER** Drawing by Saint-Exupéry in an edition of *Wind, Sand and Stars* presented to Bernard Lamotte in 1939.

**OPPOSITE** Antoine de Saint-Exupéry at his writing desk.

TERRE DES HOMMES

In 1929, he published his first book, *Southern Mail*, with Gallimard. André Beucler, a popular novelist, saw it fit to specify in his preface that Saint-Exupéry "is not a writer" and preferred to emphasize the originality of his experience. Two years later, in October 1931, Antoine released *Night Flight* to rave reviews... until awards season, when a number of critics pooh-poohed *Night Flight* as merely a pilot's narrative rather than anything resembling an authentic work of literature. The tight literary circles recognized the aviator but scorned the writer... It wasn't long before they would be proven wrong: in December of the same year, *Night Flight* was awarded the prestigious Prix Femina.

"When I am writing, I believe the book to be good. When I have finished, I believe it to be good for nothing." Saint-Exupéry doubted his legitimacy as a writer as much as his talent as an artist. He, who had never studied literature, thought it a prerequisite in order to call oneself a writer. He would tirelessly revise each sentence; he would cross out, scribble over, and cover his manuscripts with words indecipherable to anyone but himself.

## "IT'S NOT ABOUT LEARNING TO WRITE, BUT LEARNING TO SEE. WRITING IS JUST A BY-PRODUCT."

"What is writing if not correcting?" he asked himself in *The Wisdom of the Sands*. Humility is the keyword in his work. "I despise literature for literature's sake. Having really lived, I could describe real events. It's the profession that has defined the scope of my responsibility as a writer," he wrote in 1942. Writing is not an end but a means, a way to access a greater understanding of one's self and of the world. According to Saint-Exupéry, "It's not about learning to write, but learning to see. Writing is just a by-product."

Despite receiving the Grand Prix du Roman from the Académie française for *Wind, Sand and Stars*, Saint-Exupéry was ill suited for a classic novel. He gave scant priority to the plot. His books take literature down a new path: a series of instants—a strobe light of snapshots fed by his observations and his reflections on life. He wrote in fragments, which he perpetually pieced together and reworked to produce a definitive text. And what we consider of him today is not the vibrant, epic tale of his life as an aviator; rather, it is his literary achievement as a writer—a word and a statement that posterity would never call into question.

# *Saint-Exupéry and Women*

Antoine de Saint-Exupéry and women is a whole story in itself. The primary woman in his life was none other than his own mother: the only woman to whom he always remained faithful, to whom he never ceased writing, and to whom he would turn in all the difficult moments of his life. "You are the only consolation when one is sad," he wrote to her when he was twenty-two years old. "It is such security, a love like yours," he confided three years later. Widowed at the age of twenty-eight, painter and musician Marie de Fonscolombe awakened his sensibilities to literature and the magic of stories. Through his cousin Yvonne de Lestrange, Antoine would be introduced to the Paris literary scene. He would discover the young girls in flower so dear to Marcel Proust, and meet Louise de Vilmorin, his first true love.

Louise was the first in a long string of girlfriends, the ideal companions for calming his anxieties. "What I seek in a woman is someone to calm this anxiety," Saint-Exupéry wrote in 1925. When they met, she was only seventeen years old, two years younger than he was. They shared the same literary and musical tastes, and in 1923 Antoine and Louise were engaged, with the marriage set for the end of the year. Indulging his fiancée, Antoine gave up his job as a pilot. However, the engagement didn't last through autumn. Louise grew distant and her family proved hostile to Antoine. Having become an accountant in Paris, alone, and feeling lost, he drowned his melancholy and boredom in the bars in Montparnasse. In 1924, he took work as a sales representative that allowed him regular trips away into the countryside.

**ABOVE** Antoine and Consuelo at the Parisian brasserie Lipp with two journalists from *Détective* and Léon-Paul Fargue, 1934.

A two-year period of solitude ensued, during which he would make do with fleeting and unsatisfying affairs with women. He courted "a monotonous series of Colettes, Paulettes, Suzies, Daisies, and Gays, who seemed mass-produced and of whom I tired within two hours. They were waiting rooms", he wrote to his sister Marie-Madeleine. Antoine had "some desire" to get married, even if the thought of getting married scared him.

In 1929, he met Consuelo Gómez Carrillo, née Suncín-Sandoval. Consuelo was the Salvadorian widow of a Guatemalan diplomat and writer. She was a petite brunette and the same age as Antoine, whose type was more tall, blonde women, but captivated by her charm. Consuelo spoke several languages and was fanciful, artistic, and asthmatic, bohemian and eccentric, indefatigably charming, and a queen of Parisian nights. Antoine didn't wait long before proposing to her but his family was not supportive of his intended alliance with a young woman they dubbed the "drama queen" or even "usurpatrice". Antoine skirted their opinion and the couple was married in April 1931 at the church in Agay. Their relationship would prove turbulent and passionate, riddled with affairs on both sides, punctuated by break ups and reconciliations.

Consuelo possessed a talent that was dear to Antoine: she was a marvelous storyteller, just like his mother. In 1938, stopping over in Guatemala City on her way to returning to her family in El Salvador, she learned that her husband had just been admitted to a local hospital following a plane crash during an air race from New York to Punta Arenas. Despite their recent and latest breakup, Consuelo hurried to his bedside, arriving just in time to prevent the doctors from amputating his hand.

If Consuelo proved unfaithful, Antoine was hardly one to keep his distance from other women, either as confidantes or mistresses. His wife had to endure his absences, face the inherent risks of his life as an aviator, and accept the anxious waiting and solitude imposed by his missions. She had also to learn to cope with her romantic rivals, among them Nelly de Vogüé, who would write Antoine's first biography under the pseudonym Pierre Chevrier. The list goes on: from French actress Annabella to Silvia Hamilton; from Natalie Paley to Nadeja de Braganza; and all the others whose names did not survive the test of time. Yet Antoine always returned to Consuelo. For his entire life, he would remain possessed by the imperious duty of protecting her from herself and the uncertainties and hard knocks that life would deal.

**TOP LEFT** Consuelo and Antoine's wedding, April 1931.

**TOP RIGHT** Nude woman drawn in graphite and colored pencil, 1930s.

**ABOVE** Bust of a woman drawn in graphite and colored pencil, 1930s.

*"YOU ARE THE ONLY CONSOLATION WHEN ONE IS SAD."*

# Exile in America

In December 1940, following the armistice signed by France and Germany, Antoine de Saint-Exupéry set sail for New York on the ocean liner *SS Siboney*. He planned to spend several weeks in America, just time enough to convince the US to go to war alongside the Allies and propose his designs for a futuristic submarine (which he had tested himself in his bathtub!), envisaging a potential coastal invasion. The Americans took him for an eccentric, and placed him under FBI surveillance...

His books would earn him more credibility. Antoine de Saint-Exupéry became an acclaimed author: *Night Flight* sold some 250,000 copies and was adapted for the cinema with Clark Gable in the lead role. The public welcomed Saint-Exupéry as a star and American editors fussed over him. In New York, he mingled with stars like Greta Garbo, Charlie Chaplin, and Marlene Dietrich. Yet he hardly spoke a word of English, convinced that learning a foreign language posed a threat to a writer's style.

**TOP** Saint-Exupéry and Bernard Lamotte on the terrace of the painter's New York apartment.

**LEFT** In November 1942 on American radio, Saint-Exupéry called for all overseas French citizens to unite.

26

Saint-Exupéry did not enjoy living in exile. He felt uprooted. To distract himself, he played chess and entertained his entourage with his famous card tricks; he was a socialite. He drank black tea and smoked his signature Craven cigarettes. As he was wont to do, he would wake his friends in the middle of the night to read them several pages that he had just written and to ask their opinion. His editors gave him generous advances; they wanted him to extend his stay and get started on a new book. Within eight months he would write *Flight to Arras* in the hope that the text would incite the United States to enter the war. In the summer of 1942, he took up residence in Bevin House, a manor house on Long Island discovered by Consuelo, who eventually joined him there. It was while living there that he wrote *The Little Prince*, which was published in the United States the following year. Nevertheless, he longed to return to France to enlist in the fight against Nazism, despite the fact he didn't like the war, which he described as "phony adventure". "My first mistake is to be living in New York when my people are at war and dying," he wrote to his friend Silvia Hamilton. In 1943, the American authorities granted him his marching orders; he could join the fight. It was a fresh start for Saint-Exupéry.

**LEFT TO RIGHT, TOP TO BOTTOM**
Saint-Exupéry, Charlie Chaplin, Greta Garbo, Marlene Dietrich, Clark Gable...in New York, the author mingled with famous actors.

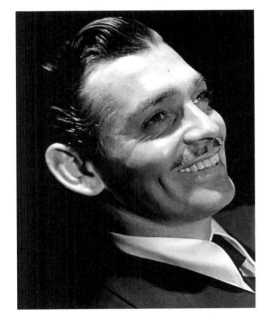

But Saint-Exupéry felt captive to the petty power games that divided the French expatriate community in New York, a mixture of partisans of the Vichy regime and supporters of De Gaulle. He called them "Fifth Avenue resistance fighters" and dreamed of an impossible harmony reconciling all the citizens of his native country. In 1942, he broadcast an appeal on American radio for the sacred union of all French citizens overseas.

# The Final Mission

Back from the United States, Antoine de Saint-Exupéry could finally taste action with the Free French Forces. He arrived in North Africa, flying his first mission in July 1943. However, his age did not work in his favor. Saint-Exupéry was forty-three years old, with a number of lingering health issues from his previous crashes. He had lived a full life of excess and sleepless nights. Even if his determination to fight remained indomitable, Antoine felt a certain weariness, a sense of being old and tired. His Lockheed P-38 Lightning was the cutting edge of American technology. He still didn't speak English, making radio contact with air traffic controllers no easy task. To compound matters further, the age limit for pilots was thirty-five years old—but he obtained an exemption from General Dwight D. Eisenhower, Commander of Allied Forces in Africa.

But Antoine could not shake his old demons. During training runs, he committed several errors that could have proven fatal. He misread his altimeter for 2,000 feet (610 meters) when in reality his altitude was at 20,000 feet (7,000 meters); on another occasion, having confused 10,000 feet with 10,000 meters, he opened the window in the canopy and the stream of air tore off his mask. On a mission over the south of France, he flew over his family château at Agay when the site held absolutely no strategic interest.

## "I'LL MEET MY END IN THE MEDITERRANEAN."

A botched landing saw his plane sent to the scrapheap and Saint-Exupéry's wings clipped. Grounded, his mood didn't improve. A psychic predicted his death was close at hand "in the waves of the sea"—had she confused his pilot's outfit with a sailor's uniform? Saint-Exupéry complained of pain in his back, head, and shoulder. He was convinced he had a fractured vertebra, lost his hair, and some teeth. Out of action and out of work, he hated everyone. Antoine was eventually reinstated to the 2/33 Group, which he rejoined in Sardinia in May 1944. But he had not flown in over eight months and his health was in a fragile state. He was incapable of putting on his flight suit without assistance and needed to don his oxygen mask the moment he got into the cockpit, chronically stricken by shortness of breath.

On July 31, 1944 at 8:35 AM, Antoine de Saint-Exupéry took off from the Borgo-Bastia airbase in Corsica after having smoked a final cigarette. "Saint-Ex" was on a reconnaissance mission over the Alps. Several hours later, he had vanished without a trace. His body was never found. "I'll meet my end in the Mediterranean," Saint-Exupéry had declared. Every hypothesis has been proposed, from his being shot down by enemy anti-aircraft fire, to a dogfight with a German pilot—the most probable—to even suicide. In September 1998, a fisherman from Marseille discovered Saint-Exupéry's identity chain bracelet. On April 7, 2004, recently discovered wreckage of a P-38 near the Island of Riou was confirmed by French authorities as coming from Saint-Exupéry's plane. Four years later, German pilot Horst Rippert claimed to recall having shot down the plane on July 31, 1944. Antoine de Saint-Exupéry was forty-four years old.

2- The Origins of
The Little Prince

# Biographical and Personal Sources

The story of *The Little Prince* did not appear out of thin air in the middle of the desert like its protagonist did. The tale finds its origins in the writer's life story. It was fed by his experiences, his encounters, and his childhood memories.

The desert plays a fundamental role in the genesis of the work. Saint-Exupéry first laid eyes on it between Casablanca and Dakar on his first flight over Africa, which he made in tandem with another pilot in the company, René Riguelle. Henri Guillaumet flew with them in convoy. Their mission came to an early end when their engine threw a rod and they made a crash landing in the sand. Whereas Riguelle would climb aboard and continue on in Guillaumet's Breguet, Antoine was left behind for the night, awaiting rescue armed with a pair of pistols. This would portend the aviator in *The Little Prince*, sitting in the Sahara at the foot of his broken-down aircraft, "more isolated than a shipwrecked sailor on a raft in the middle of the ocean." Saint-Exupéry would also evoke this episode in *Wind, Sand and Stars*: "I lay there pondering my situation, lost in the desert and in danger, naked between sky and sand, withdrawn by too much silence from the poles of my life. I knew that I should wear out days and weeks returning to them if I were not sighted by some plane, or if the next day the Moors did not find and murder me. Here I possessed nothing in the world. I was no more than a mortal strayed between sand and stars, conscious of the single blessing of breathing..."

*"I POSSESSED NOTHING IN THE WORLD. I WAS NO MORE THAN A MORTAL STRAYED BETWEEN SAND AND STARS, CONSCIOUS OF THE SINGLE BLESSING OF BREATHING..."*

In December 1935, while taking part in an air race between Paris and Saigon, Saint-Exupéry crashed in the Libyan desert. He spent three days with his flight engineer, André Prévot, wandering through the sands in scorching heat. With their water supplies exhausted, death looked certain for the two men. They were saved by a Bedouin caravan that seemed to appear out of nowhere, in the same way that the little prince appears to the aviator.

Some of the tale's characters find their roots in Saint-Exupéry's memories. The fox is reminiscent of the fennec that he tamed when he was posted in Cape Juby. The snake was inspired by his time spent in Argentina. The baobabs recall his stopovers in Senegal, when he regularly flew the route between Casablanca and Dakar. The lamplighter was not simply a figment of his imagination: the young Antoine met him "for real," during his vacations in Saint-Maurice-de-Rémens. As for the businessman, perhaps we might see him in Marcel Bouilloux-Lafont, the entrepreneur who added the Toulouse to Saint-Louis (Senegal) route to Latécoère's postal lines, and who created Aéropostale.

According to Nelly de Vogüé, the little prince character may have been inspired by Pierre Sudreau. As a young twelve-year-old boy, he was known to wear a little prince-like scarf; Saint-Exupéry, who had taken him under his wing, nicknamed Sudreau "the little Pierre".

The Little Prince is also borne of the stories his mother used to tell him and the books he read as a child. Novels such as *The Lamplighter* by Maria Cummins or *Le Pays des 36 000 volontés* (*The Land of 36,000 Wishes*) by André Maurois (who presented Antoine a personal copy), are other possible influences. So, too, perhaps *L'Homme de la pampa* (*The Man from the Pampas*) by Jules Supervielle, which opens with an epigraph summing up the spirit of *The Little Prince*: "Dreams and realities, farce, anxiety—I wrote this short novel for the child I once was, and who asked me for stories."

Saint-Exupéry himself presaged his future work in *Wind, Sand and Stars*. As well as allusions to desert, volcanoes, and kingdoms—all elements found in *The Little Prince*—he describes encountering an innocent but impoverished young boy with his parents: "Little princes in legends are no different from this."

**PREVIOUS SPREAD** A sketch of the Little Prince, looking slightly irritated…

**OPPOSITE PAGE** Pierre-Georges Latécoère, founder of the Compagnie générale aéropostale.

**ABOVE** After crashing in the Libyan desert, Saint-Exupéry and his mechanic-navigator, André Prévot, wandered through the desert for three days before being rescued by Bedouins.

**BOTTOM LEFT** Politician Pierre Sudreau, nicknamed "the little Pierre" by Saint-Exupéry, may have inspired the latter's character of the little prince.

**LEFT** Loyal friend, intellectual companion, and friend of heart Nelly de Vogüé, who wrote the first biography of Saint-Exupéry under the pseudonym Pierre Chevrier.

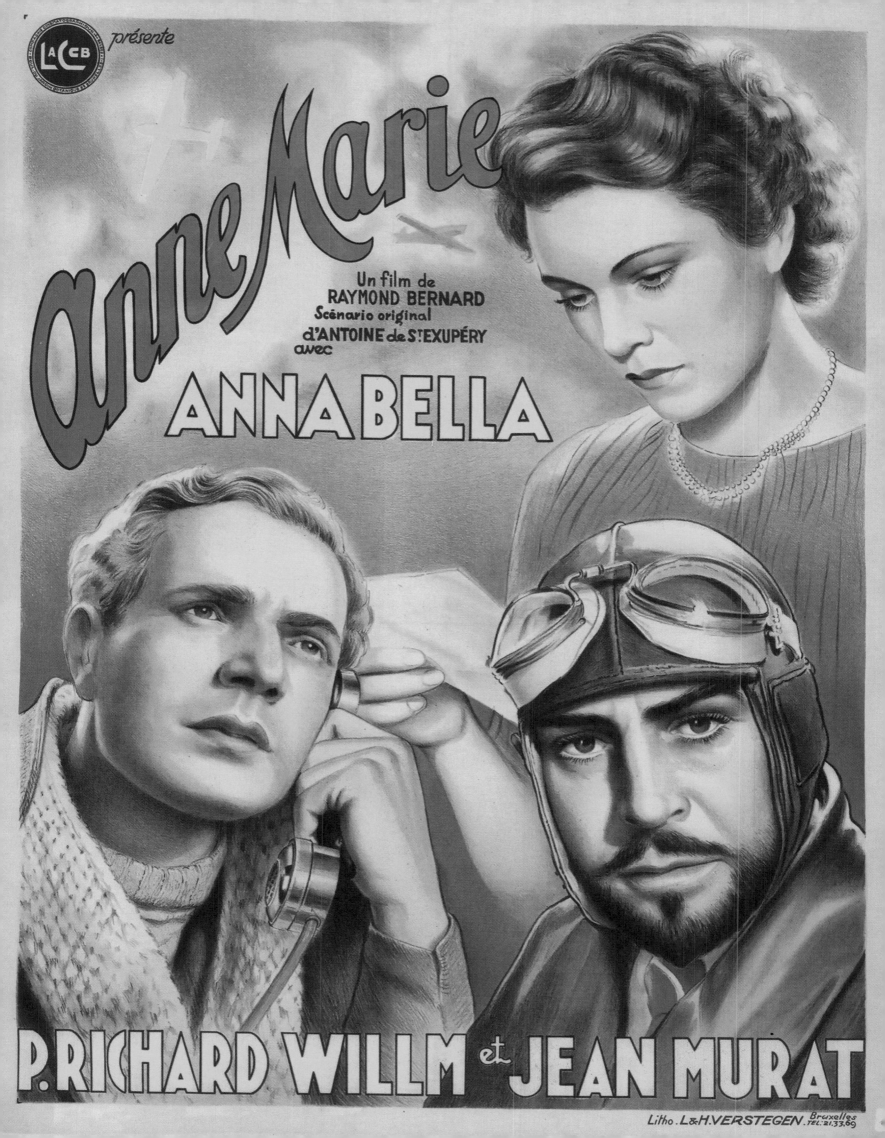

# The Little Prince, an Editor's Request

To whom can we credit the inspiration behind *The Little Prince*? Determining the exact origin of the book is no easy task, as the claims to its paternity are numerous. In 1942, while dining with Saint-Exupéry at Le Café Arnold in New York, publisher Eugene Reynal's wife Elizabeth was fascinated by the "little fellow" that he sketched as he spoke. Reynal and his associate Curtice Hitchcock had just published *Wind, Sand and Stars*. Earlier, in 1934, the two men had published the novel *Mary Poppins* by Pamela Travers. Hoping for another such success, they proposed that Saint-Exupéry submit them a book also aimed at young readers. "Saint-Ex" was intrigued by the idea. His publishers imagined a Christmas story that they could have on bookshelves in time for the winter holidays. A contract was signed in November with a paid advance of $3,000. All that was left to do was for Antoine to start writing...

Other acquaintances of the writer maintain having played a role in the genesis of *The Little Prince*. His New York companion Silvia Hamilton believed that it was while staying with her that Saint-Exupéry drew inspiration in conceiving his characters. Her poodle resembled a sheep; her boxer Hannibal looked a tiger; and one of her blond-haired dolls could bring to mind a little prince. French actress Annabella recalled how the idea of writing a tale came to Saint-Exupéry while they were reading through Andersen's *The Little Mermaid* together. Painter Hedda Sterne, seeing his habit of drawing his little fellow anywhere and everywhere, suggested that he illustrate the book himself. Saint-Exupéry had first envisaged calling on his painter friend Bernard Lamotte, who he had met at the École de Beaux-Arts and who had illustrated *Flight to Arras*. But Lamotte's first sketches were too realistic, too dark,

and not "naive" enough; Saint-Exupéry wasn't convinced. Several acquaintances of his, such as film director René Clair claimed to have given "Saint-Ex" his art supplies. Explorer Paul-Émile Victor claimed to have introduced Antoine to watercolor pencils, but this is hardly enough—indeed a far cry from it—to take credit for inspiring the story itself, all the more given that Saint-Exupéry himself acquired all the materials he needed from a local New York drugstore...

But perhaps we should not look any further for the origins of *The Little Prince* than Antoine de Saint-Exupéry himself: his spellbound memory of the stories his mother would read him when he was a child, and the admiration he felt for fairy tales. "We know full well that fairy tales are life's only truth," he would write in *Lettres à l'inconnue* (*Letters to Madame X*).

# Léon Werth, the "Best Friend"

*The Little Prince* is dedicated to Léon Werth. The dedication is prefaced by a short text in which Saint-Exupéry describes Werth as "the best friend I have in the world" and as a "grown-up [who] understands everything, even books about children". This leads Saint-Exupéry to refine his inscription, eventually dedicating the story "To Léon Werth when he was a little boy".

At once novelist, journalist, essayist, and art critic, Léon Werth was also an anti-militant and anti-colonial pacifist libertarian. To be as free-thinking in as many ways was quite uncommon—and quite unpopular—in France in the interbellum period. Saint-Exupéry pays homage to Werth in *Letter to a Hostage*.

Originally, *Letter to a Hostage* was intended to be the preface to Werth's *33 Days*, a personal written account of his exodus from Paris in 1940 as the Nazis took over. Werth gave the manuscript to Saint-Exupéry for editing as the pilot left for New York. The preface, first entitled *Letter to a Friend*, then *Letter to Léon Werth*, evolved to its final incarnation for the sake of protecting Werth, who, as a Jew hiding from the Nazis in the Jura mountains, embodied France under German occupation. *Letter to a Hostage* was published by Saint-Exupéry in 1943. While directly addressing his friend, Antoine was also conveying a message to the entire French population who, like Werth, had been taken hostage.

In 1948, Léon Werth would write a book called *Saint-Exupéry, tel que je l'ai connu* (*Saint-Exupéry as I Knew Him*) in which he paid homage to the author of *The Little Prince*, declaring, "Not only did he possess the ability to charm children, but also to persuade grown-ups that they were as majestic as the characters in fairy tales. Saint-Exupéry had always remained young at heart."

> *"I ASK THE INDULGENCE OF THE CHILDREN WHO MAY READ THIS BOOK FOR DEDICATING IT TO A GROWN-UP. I HAVE A SERIOUS REASON: HE IS THE BEST FRIEND I HAVE IN THE WORLD."*

*"THIS GROWN-UP LIVES IN FRANCE WHERE HE IS HUNGRY AND COLD. HE NEEDS CHEERING UP."*

**THESE PAGES** Léon Werth, Saint-Exupéry's "best friend in the world" to whom he dedicated *The Little Prince*. Saint-Exupéry also paid homage to him in *Letter to a Hostage*.

# Sketches of the Little Prince

Long before his "official" birth in 1943, the little prince had already taken shape in numerous doodles and sketches. Even if he was never designated as such or if his form was not always identical to that which was immortalized in the story, the physical resemblance to our hero is striking. Antoine de Saint-Exupéry had always drawn little characters. They can be found on all sorts of scraps of paper: on loose sheets, receipts, school workbooks, tablecloths and restaurant menus, diaries and manuscripts. Sometimes the little men stand on blossoming flowerbeds, just like the little prince on his planet.

At the start of WWII, when Antoine was called up, the author drew himself in a letter addressed to Léon Werth, standing on a cloud as if suspended above the Earth that looked very much like the future asteroid B 612.

**ABOVE** A "star tree", drawn in the margin of one of the writer's manuscripts

**THESE PAGES** Before creating the little prince, Saint-Exupéry imagined numerous little characters that foreshadowed the immortal protagonist.

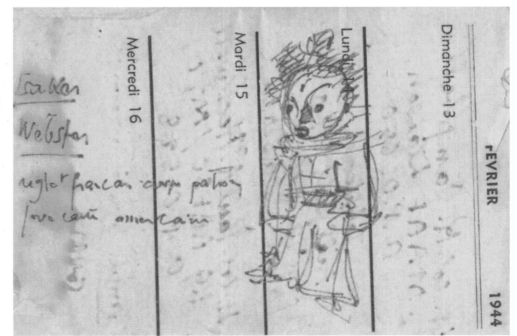

Another drawing, given to his friend Nelly de Vogüé, shows a ranting character standing on what looks like a planet. According to specialists on Saint-Exupéry's drawings, the undated sketch was drawn at the end of the 1930s or the start of the 1940s.

The incarnation of the little prince as we know him didn't magically appear out of nowhere, a sudden figment of the writer-illustrator's imagination. Rather, he was the result of a creative process, the fruit of a long development on the part of his creator, who continued to enjoy doodling for as long as he lived.

**ABOVE RIGHT** Saint-Exupéry scrawls one of his little characters on a letter bearing the logo of Aéropostale.

**ABOVE** These roses adorn *L'Adieu*, one of five poems by Saint-Exupéry collected in an illustrated, calligraphed notebook in 1919.

# The Manuscript and Proof Sets

The original manuscript of *The Little Prince*, donated by Silvia Hamilton, can be found in the Morgan Library & Museum in New York. Four other typewritten versions exist, in which Antoine de Saint-Exupéry made various additions and corrections. One is in Austin, Texas; the author had sent it to his favorite translator, Lewis Galantière, who was unable to work on *The Little Prince* because of an airplane accident. Another belongs to the French national library, a gift from pianist Nadia Boulanger, who had received it as a present from Saint-Exupéry. A third, whose provenance is unknown, was sold in London in 1989 by Sotheby's. The last of the four is said to be the property of an heir of Consuelo.

**ABOVE** An unpublished picture of the little prince sitting on his planet with his back to the viewer, 1942.

**RIGHT** Two sketches of the little prince on a letter composed by "St-Ex", date and provenance unknown.

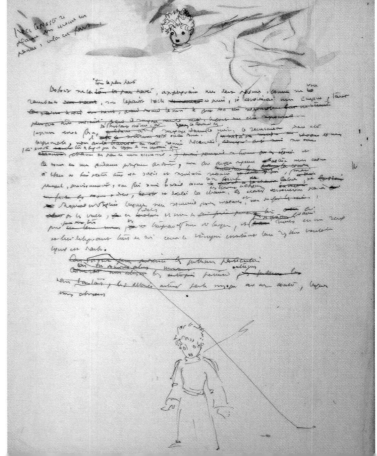

A proof set (in publishing terms, the first printing of a book intended for proofreading and quality control and not intended for sale), supposedly having belonged to French actress Annabella, was bought at auction by a collector. And a typescript version identical to the published version was bequeathed to the French Air & Space Museum in Le Bourget.

All of these texts are a precious aid in shedding light on the context in which *The Little Prince* was created: Antoine de Saint-Exupéry left nothing behind that could otherwise help us understand his method of working or his sources of inspiration. The only clue he left is a few words in his *Carnets* (*Notebooks*): "Method. Reread books from childhood, entirely forgetting the naive part which has no effect at all, but instead noting all along the prayers, and the concepts conveyed by that imagery." These different versions of the manuscript show diverse modifications between them, in the form of additions or variations as well as drawings that were omitted from the final version. The copy sold by Sotheby's contains more than 100 of the author's own written corrections. They are testament to the genesis of the work and teach us about Saint-Exupéry's process of trial and error while writing, helping to comprehend the creative process behind *The Little Prince*.

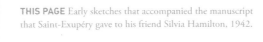

**THIS PAGE** Early sketches that accompanied the manuscript that Saint-Exupéry gave to his friend Silvia Hamilton, 1942.

The Little Prince

ANTOINE DE SAINT-EXUPÉRY

*"I believe that for his escape he took advantage of the migration of a flock of wild birds."*

The Little P

WRITTEN AND DRAW

ANTOINE DE SAINT

TRANSLATED FROM THE FRENCH BY K

REYNAL & HITCHCOCK

# 3- The Little Prince, the Oeuvre

# First Editions

Aside from one or two misprints and imperfections, this version also contains some notable differences to the original in the text as well as the illustrations. Asteroid 325 becomes asteroid 3251 and the little prince witnesses 43 sunsets, rather than the original 44. According to one of the typescripts, Saint-Exupéry seems to have deliberated over this number of sunsets elsewhere as well. Nor are the drawings all identical: the little prince's royal costume changes from green to blue, while the star on the horizon of the astronomer's telescope has disappeared.

The first edition of *The Little Prince* was published by Reynal & Hitchcock in New York on April 6, 1943, both in English and French (as *Le Petit Prince*). 525 copies of the English version were printed, numbered, and signed by the author (of which 25 copies were not intended for sale), whereas 260 copies of the French version were printed (of which 10 were not intended for sale). This first edition has 91 numbered pages, with a salmon-colored hardcover and a dust jacket that shows the little prince on the asteroid B 612.

A standard version, unsigned by Saint-Exupéry and priced at $2.00, was then published in an identical format, with just one difference: there was no print notice. Much prized by collectors and bibliophiles, the signed first edition books sold for between 20,000 and 25,000 euro in 2013, whereas standard edition copies sold for a tenth of the price.

In April 1946, two years after Saint-Exupéry's death, *The Little Prince* was published posthumously in France. Extracts of the text were printed earlier as pull-out supplements in the second issue of the French weekly *Elle* in November 1945. Produced by Gallimard, this 93-page edition sold 12,750 copies (of which 300, numbered I to CCC, were not intended for sale). Its dark blue clothbound hardcover featured a depiction of the American cover art in red, over the NRF (for *Nouvelle Revue française*) logo of Gallimard editions.

*PREVIOUS PAGES* An original manuscript of *The Little Prince* belongs to the Morgan Library, New York.

*LEFT* The clothbound hardcover of the first edition.

*ABOVE* *The Little Prince* in the Morgan Library.

*"IT MOVES ME TO THINK THAT MY MOTHER LIVED IN THE SAME BUILDING WHERE SAINT-EXUPÉRY WROTE* THE LITTLE PRINCE. *IF NOTHING ELSE, I AM MOVED BY THE FACT THAT SHE HAD NO IDEA THAT THE BOOK WAS BEING WRITTEN, NO IDEA WHO THE AUTHOR WAS."*
— PAUL AUSTER

# French and French-Language Editions

By the end of June 1946, only two months after its French publication, *The Little Prince* had sold nearly 10,000 copies. But it was only on November 12, 1947 that Gallimard would reprint the novel, this time in paperback. A number of reasons were behind the delay, primarily the lawsuit between the French publisher and Reynal & Hitchcock regarding shared rights to the book. Additionally, obtaining materials at the end of WWII made publishing difficult and Gallimard was unable to print as many volumes as they would have liked. Lastly, it was necessary to find common ground with the representatives of Saint-Exupéry's numerous successors—his wife, mother, and sisters—whose individual interests could be quite different.

*"TODAY I THINK THAT THE LITTLE PRINCE IS A GREAT, BEAUTIFUL BOOK, A SINCERE AND DAZZLING BOOK, A MOMENT OF GRACE. BUT I ALSO THINK IT HAS LITTLE TO DO WITH CHILDHOOD. THE PRINCE MAY WELL BE LITTLE, BUT HE IS NEITHER CHILD NOR BOY, NOR GIRL. HE IS JUST A SOUL. OF COURSE, EVERYONE CAN READ A BOOK ABOUT A SOUL. INCLUDING CHILDREN."*
— *MARIE DESPLECHIN*

The paperback, made available in bookshops for the end-of-year holidays, was printed in a run of 11,000 copies. Several months later, in February 1948, another print run followed of 22,000 copies. From July 1947 to June 1948, more than 23,000 copies were sold. From then on, the book's popularity had been established and never looked back: *The Little Prince* has been the most popular book in France for young people, even if Saint-Exupéry did not intend it to be a children's book. By 1958, the paperback edition had been reprinted nineteen times, each run varying in volume between 22,000 and 55,000 copies. Total sales surpassed 450,000 copies.

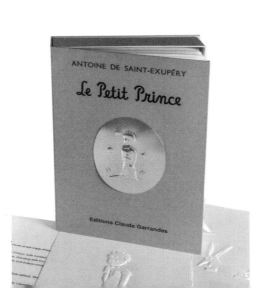

**CLOCKWISE, FROM TOP LEFT** *The Little Prince* from Gallimard's Albums Junior collection; the anniversary boxed set included the book, a CD audiobook read by actor Gérard Philipe, and a DVD; a "pop-up" version of *The Little Prince* brought the settings to life; the first edition of the story in Braille with Saint-Exupéry's illustrations in relief (published by Claude Garrandes).

By the early 1980s, *The Little Prince* had sold some 2 million copies in both its original and its luxury editions. However, from this decade on, the book's success reached another dimension. The Gallimard editions of *The Little Prince* multiplied. Until the end of the 1970s, the book was available in four versions: the original in paperback, the 1951 luxury hardcover edition by bookbinder Paul Bonet, a 1952 book club edition, and the 1953 publication in Gallimard's prestigious Bibliothèque de la Pléiade series. In September 1979, the first children's paperback edition was released under the Folio Junior label. Some 20 years later, in February 1999, the work was finally published under the Folio label, Gallimard's renowned paperback collection for adults—proof of the universality of the tale.
And Saint-Exupéry's celebrity gained currency in France in 1993, when the newly released 50-franc note featured images of both the little prince and his creator.

In 60 years, *The Little Prince* has sold over 11 million copies in France, more than half of which were in paperback.

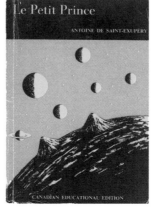

**TOP TO BOTTOM, LEFT TO RIGHT**

Dar El Maaref, Sousse, 2003.
Reynal & Hitchcock, New York, 1943.
Kapo, Moscow, 2010.
Éditions Gallimard, Paris, 1948.
Harcourt, New York, 1954.
Éditions Gallimard, Paris, 1948, hardcover with a slipcase.
Svenska Bokförlaget, Stockholm, 1958.
Izdatelstvo "Vuschaia Skola", Moscow, 1966.
Bellhaven House Limited, Scarborough, 1973.
Jasikach, Moscow, 1960.

# An Unpublished Chapter

The original manuscript of *The Little Prince* kept at the Morgan Library & Museum includes an unpublished chapter. Scrawled in Saint-Exupéry's characteristically tiny, almost illegible handwriting, the chapter provides an account of the little prince's encounter with a crossword enthusiast. This man explains to the little prince that for three days, he has been searching for a word: six letters; starts with "G"; means, "gargling".

---

"This is a strange planet," the little prince said to himself as he traveled on.

He had left the desert and headed straight for the Himalayas. For so long, he had wanted to see a real mountain! He had three volcanoes, but they only came up to his knee. He would often lean on the dormant one, but that was barely like a stool.

"From a mountain as high as this one," he said to himself, "I shall be able to see the whole planet at one glance, and all the people..."

But he had not seen anything apart from pointy granite spikes and large, yellow landslides. If you gathered all the inhabitants of this planet and got them to stand upright and somewhat crowded together, as they do for some big public assembly: whites, blacks, Asians, young, old, women, and men— without missing out a single one—all of humanity would fit into the [Author's note: illegible word] on Long Island. If you took a [primary school globe] and poked a hole in that globe with a needle, all humanity could live on the area covered by the pinhole. Of course,

*"WHERE ARE THE MEN?" THOUGHT THE LITTLE PRINCE WHILE TRAVELING.*

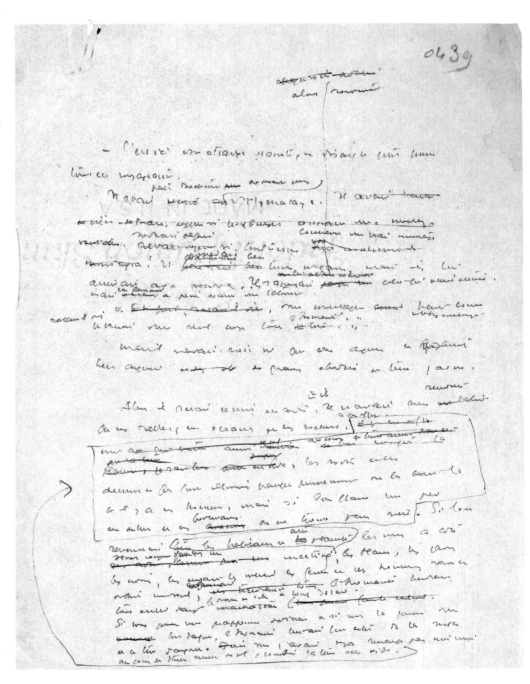

in three years of flying, I myself had already noticed how empty the Earth is. And in fact, highways and railways create an illusion of the opposite precisely because they are built in the places where people live, but if you wander a little beyond these boulevards, there is nothing to be found.

But I had never paid much attention when I thought about that. It's thanks to the little prince that I have given it more detailed consideration.

"Where are the men?" thought the little prince while traveling. He met the first person on a road. "Aha! Now I can find out what they think about life on this planet," he said to himself. "Perhaps this is an ambassador of the human spirit..."

"Good morning," he said to him cheerfully.
"Good morning," said the man.
"What are you doing?" said the little prince.
"I am very busy," said the man.

"Of course he is very busy," said the little prince to himself. "He lives on such a large planet. There is so much to do." He almost didn't dare disturb the man.

"Perhaps I can help you," he said to him all the same: the little prince would have liked to be helpful.

"Perhaps," the man said to him. "I have been working for three days without success. I am looking for a word, six letters long, that starts with 'G' and means, 'gargling'."

"Gargling," said the little prince.
"Gargling," said the man.

# *Variations of the Text*

Careful reading of the different versions of the manuscript (no small feat given Saint-Exupéry's almost indecipherable handwriting) proves fascinating: they present several notable variations from the definitive text.

## BOAT OR POTATO?

The narrator's drawing of an elephant swallowed by a boa had been preceded by an illustration that Saint-Exupéry abandoned, unhappy with the final result. It was revealed when it was sold in 1986:

> *I don't know how to draw. I tried twice to draw a boat and a friend asked me if it was a potato.*

## MANHATTAN

In Chapter 17, Antoine de Saint-Exupéry imagines assembling the Earth's population on one island in the Pacific Ocean.

> *If the two billion inhabitants who people its surface were all to stand upright and somewhat crowded together, as they do for some big public assembly, they could easily be put into one public square twenty miles long and twenty miles wide. All humanity could be piled up on a small Pacific islet.*

In a first draft of the manuscript, he had considered assembling humanity in Manhattan, where he wrote the story.

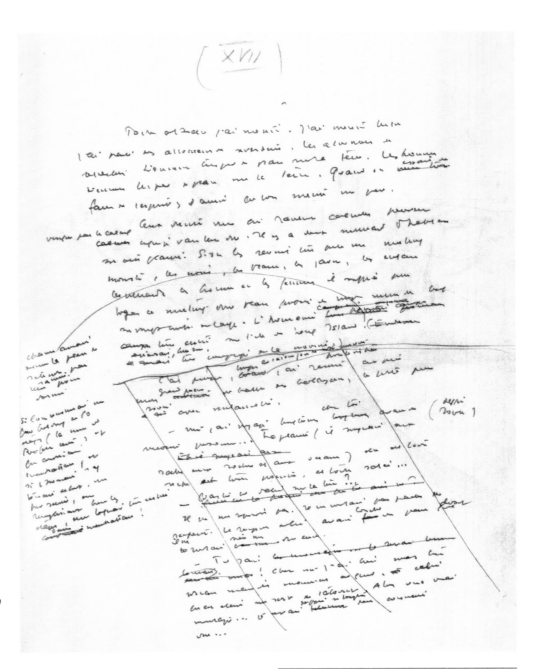

*If Manhattan were covered in fifty-story buildings and if people, standing upright and crowded together, filled all the floors of these buildings, all of humanity could live in Manhattan.*

**THIS CHAPTER** Original manuscript pages of these variations, as well as two unpublished watercolors.

## THE HILLSIDE

Chapter 20, in which the encounter between the little prince and the roses takes place, originally started as follows:

*A hillside is a lovely thing. It's the loveliest thing we have. A mountain is always arrogant, a planet is often sad, but a hill is welcoming and gay. The side of a hill is always full of pretty things that look like toys: apple trees in blossom, sheep, fir trees like those at Christmas. The little prince, quite surprised, slowly walked down the slope of the hill until he came upon a garden, and in this garden were five thousand flowers.*

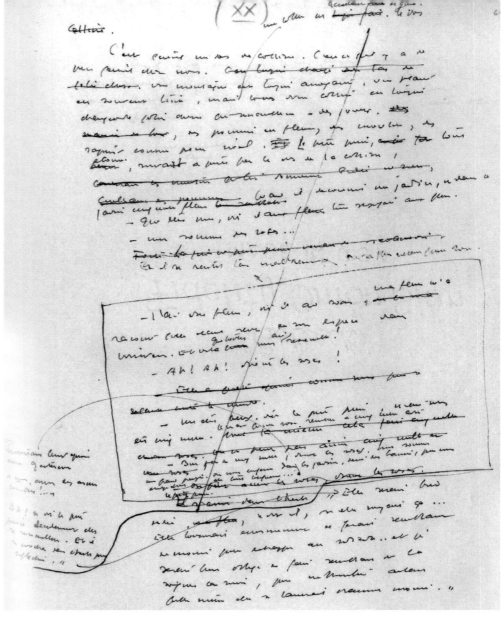

*"A HILLSIDE IS
A LOVELY THING.
IT'S THE LOVELIEST
THING WE HAVE."*

*"WHO ARE YOU?"*
*SAID THE MAN. "WHAT*
*DO YOU WANT?"*
*"A FRIEND," SAID THE*
*LITTLE PRINCE.*

**DINNER, INTERRUPTED**
Chapter 25 would have been followed
by this passage and the little prince's
meeting with the merchant.

*"Good morning," said the little prince.*
*"Who are you?" said the*
*man. "What do you want?"*
*"A friend," said the little prince.*

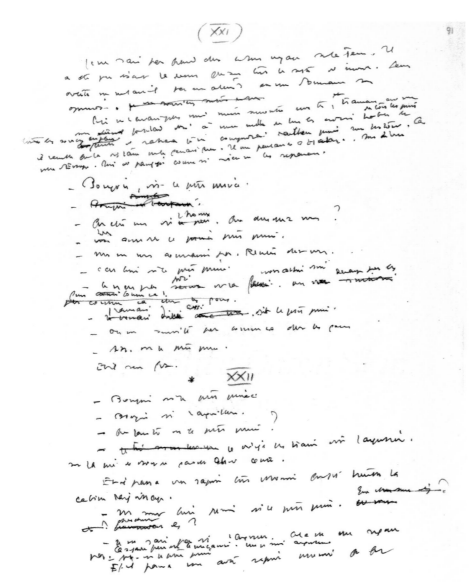

*"We do not know each other.*
*Go home."*
*"It is far away," said the little prince.*
*"This is not funny," said the woman.*
*"You cannot disturb people like this!"*
*"I would have eaten, too," said the*
*little prince.*
*"You cannot invite yourself to*
*someone's house like that."*
*"Ah," said the little prince.*

*And he went away.*

The following scene seems to be a more
developed version of the previous draft.

*"Good morning," said the little prince.*

*He stood up and smiled in the*
*doorway to the dining room of*
*a house he had chosen that was the*
*same as the others. The man and*
*the woman turned toward him and*
*said to the light of his smile:*

*"Who are you?" said the*
*man. "What do you want?"*
*"I would like to sit down," said the*
*little prince.*
*"We do not know each other.*
*Go home."*
*"It is far away," said the little prince.*
*"You are impolite," said the woman.*
*"We are about to eat. You cannot*
*disturb people like this."*
*"I would have eaten too," said the*
*little prince.*
*"You cannot invite yourself to*
*someone's house like that."*
*"Ah," said the little prince.*

*And he went away.*

*"They do not even know," he said to*
*himself, "that they are looking for*
*something."*

## THE VISIT TO THE MERCHANT

This is the second text that was originally intended to follow chapter 25. In the merchant character, Saint-Exupéry had prepared an acerbic critique of consumer society, using him to touch on themes such as freedom, the economics of supply and demand, and saving time. Afterward, it would seem as though this merchant was reduced to selling pills.

*At the Merchant's:*

*"Ah, a customer!"*

*"Good morning.
What is that?"*

*"That? It is a very expensive instrument. Turn the handle, and it makes the sound of an earthquake..."*

*"What is it for?"*

*"It is for people who like earthquakes."*

*"I do not like them."*

*"Hum! Hum! If you do not like earthquakes, I cannot sell you my instrument. Industry and commerce will be paralyzed. Here is a book on advertising. After you have studied it well, you will like earthquakes and you will hurry back to buy my instrument. It is full of easy-to-remember slogans."*

*"But what if I want an instrument to read the book?"*

*"There is no such thing. That is disorder. You are a revolutionary.*

*An instrument must be liked. If you do not like what is offered you, you will never be happy. If you like what is offered you, you will be happy. What's more, you will be a free citizen."*

*"How so?"*

*"You will only be free to buy when something you want is offered you. Without this, you are creating disorder. Go read the lesson in the advertising book."*

*"Why are you selling that?" said the little prince.*

*"It saves a tremendous amount of time," said the merchant. "Computations have been made by experts. You save twenty-six minutes in every week."*

*"And what do you do with those twenty-six minutes?"*

*"Anything you like," said the merchant.*

*"If I had twenty-six minutes to spend as I like," said the little prince, "do you know what I would do?"*

*"No," said the merchant.*

*"I would walk at my leisure towards a spring of fresh water..."*

*"That is worthless," said the merchant.*

53

## THE VISIT TO THE INVENTOR

There are other encounters between men and the little prince that the author chose to leave out of the final draft. The following "Visit to the Inventor," might be read as a thinly-veiled critique of America, for which, with the exception of New York, Saint-Exupéry felt a certain coldness.

*"Good morning," said the little prince.*

*"Good morning," said the inventor of electric servants. Before him was a magnificent board covered in electronic buttons of every color.*

*"What are all those buttons for?" asked the little prince.*

*"They save time," said the inventor, who was covered in awards. "If you are cold, you press this button here and it warms you up. If you are too hot, you press this button here and it cools you down. If you like bowling, you must love watching the pins fall: press this button here and all the pins fall down at once. If you like smoking, press this orange button, and you will find a lit cigarette placed right between your lips. But smoking takes up time: one hundred and ten minutes a week. So you can press the purple button, and a well-built robot will smoke the cigarette for*

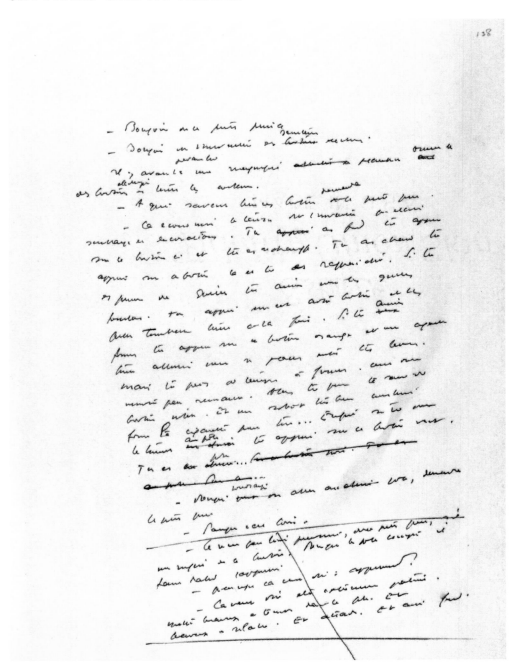

you... Finally, if you want to go to the poles, press this green button, and you will find yourself there..."

"Why would I want to go there?" asked the little prince.

"Because they are far away."

The following is crossed out:

"It is not far for me," said the little prince, "if all I need is this button. For the poles to be worth anything, they must be tamed first."

"What does that mean: 'tamed'?"

"It means being extremely patient, and putting a lot of time into the pole. And a lot of silence."

## CONCLUSION
Lastly, Saint-Exupéry wrote a conclusion to *The Little Prince* that he decided not to keep:

As I am indulgent, I never told grown-ups that I am not one of theirs. I hid from them the fact that I was always five or six years old at heart. I also hid my drawings from them. But I would like to show them to my friends. These drawings are my memories.

# The Little Prince on Earth: Translations

Available in more than 270 languages and dialects and transcribed into 26 different alphabets, *The Little Prince* is the most translated literary work in the world after the Bible, the reigning champion with 2,000 languages. Even *Harry Potter*, magic and all, could not surpass *The Little Prince*: J.K. Rowling's novel is "only" available in 60 languages. But accurately keeping track of the available editions—around 600—well as the number of copies sold—30 million according to some sources, 80 according to others—is truly mission impossible.

Saint-Exupéry's text was first adapted into Polish in 1947. Until 1990, some 20 new translations came out every decade. After that, this figure doubled. In 2000, the centenary year of the author's birth, a new version appeared every month. The rediscovery of European regional languages contributed to the increase in the number of these translations. At first, distribution was limited to western and northern Europe. Then in the 1950s, *The Little Prince* spread to Africa and Asia, finding particular popularity in Japan. Also in the former Eastern bloc, where the multiplicity of translations preceded the sudden opening of the borders, as in former Yugoslavia. Today, *The Little Prince* is available in more diverse languages: Amharic, in Ethiopia; Dari, in Iran; the Amazigh languages of Morocco; Kannada, in India; Quechua in Peru; Urdu in Pakistan; and Esperanto. Not to mention the "counterfeit" editions: despite their contraband status, these works, condemned though they may be by Western law, contribute to broadening *The Little Prince*'s audience.

ANTOINE DE SAINT-EXUPÉRY

# SO SHIỸAXAUOLEC NTA'A

*Le Petit Prince*

Sometimes, translators are restricted by cultural as well as linguistic barriers. In Toba, an indigenous language spoken by an aboriginal community in northern Argentina, no concept exists of a "prince". On the other hand, Saint-Exupéry's dialogue with the fox and the snake fits perfectly into the Toba people's world vision, and *The Little Prince* has been available in their language since 2005. As for the Moroccan translator who took on the challenge of translating the story into Amazigh, he was confronted with serious difficulties in finding equivalent terms such as "reverberate" and "tie", and notions like boredom or absurdity...

삼성 세계 명작 ★ 저학년

# 어린왕자

## The Little Prince

원작 생 텍쥐페리 엮음 유효진 그림 방정화

삼성출판사
samsungbooks.com

*I BÈLE STORIE*

# 'L PRÌNCEP PICINÌ

*A cura di Margherita Recanati*

## LEONARDO FACCO EDITORE

ROYAUME DU MAROC
INSTITUT ROYAL
DE LA CULTURE AMAZIGHE

Centre des Etudes Artistiques, des Expressions
Littéraires et de la Production Audiovisuelle

ANTOINE DE SAINT-EXUPÉRY

# *Quyllur llaqtayuq wawamanta*

Qillqaqpa dibuhunkunantin

Frances simimanta tikraqkuna
LYDIA CORNEJO ENDARA - CÉSAR ITIER

# The Little Prince on Earth: Illustrations

Certain foreign editions of *The Little Prince* offer unexpected adaptations for of Saint-Exupéry's illustrations. Most feature one of the story's two most famous drawings on their covers: either the little prince on asteroid B 612 with his hands in his pockets; or the full-length portrait of him dressed in his cape with his sword in his hand. Other covers feature the little prince's flight with a group of wild birds. But the number of changes made to this mythical scene are numerous: the colors of the planet and those of Saint-Exupéry's hero's pants are not always the same; stars and planets are added to the background; the protagonist's shape at times modified to the point of being unrecognizable... Some of the drawings on the inside pages have also been radically altered.

**THIS CHAPTER** More than 150 covers of *The Little Prince* throughout the world.

While the versions published in the West endeavor to remain as true to Saint-Exupéry's oeuvre as possible, foreign editions allow themselves a broad license that some might find surprising. "On the one hand, there is tradition. On the other, there is variety. Here, there is a heritage of identity; there, unconstrained adaptation," writes historian and archivist Alban Cerisier in *Il était une fois… « Le Petit Prince »* (*Once upon a time, "The Little Prince"*). But these interpretations should not be seen as indifference toward the original. Rather, they translate differences from Western legal norms, which are concerned with the notion of intellectual property and the author's intent. They may also express another relationship between the text and the illustrators: this varies according to culture, and as such allows for a greater liberty in interpretation. In other cases, considerations of production costs and budgets can distance publishers from the original. Some must make do with black and white illustrations, others have to get rid of all cover art in the name of less expensive printing. Since *The Little Prince* is a book with a universal audience, it is necessary to accept that other cultures will appropriate and adapt the work according to their own traditions.

世上最美的故事

小王子
STORY BOOK

文：聖修伯里　圖：金珉志

真正重要的東西，用眼睛是看不見的。

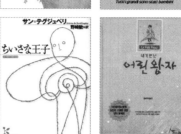

# Critical Reception

When it was first published, *The Little Prince* received enthusiastic reviews from most literary critics, although it did perplex others. Is it a children's story, as Saint-Exupéry's dedication to Léon Werth would have us believe? Or is this story really more of a philosophical tale aimed at adults, whose mysterious meaning is meant to be accessible to "grown-ups"? After all, as Saint-Exupéry notes in his dedication, "all grown-ups were once children—although few of them remember it."

German philosopher Martin Heidegger wrote on the cover of the 1949 German edition of *The Little Prince* that it was the most important French work of the century. A far cry from the cruel words of French philosopher, writer, and journalist Jean-François Revel in 1965, who described Saint-Exupéry's work as "cockpit imbecility masquerading as wisdom," in which "verbose inanity becomes profound philosophical truth by virtue of taking off from the ground..."

> "One of those legendary characters...the way that children like them."
> **Yvette Jeandet**,
> *Les Nouvelles littéraires*

> "The work is... among the most audacious books for children."
> **Paul Bodin**,
> *Combat*

> "*The Little Prince* is Saint-Exupéry—the child that he was and that he remained in spite of grown-ups; it's the son he could have had and no doubt wanted; it's also the young friend who lets himself be tamed and then disappears. It's his childhood and the world's childhood: provisions of sweetness, discovered and rediscovered in the beloved desert."
> **Adrienne Monnier,**
> publisher of the *Navire d'argent*

> "A story for children, or rather, to use the author's own distinction, for the children we once were. A story full of poetry, kindness, wisdom, and creativity."
> **Clara Malraux**,
> *Paysage dimanche*

> "The book's great artistry lies in creating this little prince with such care and such tenderness that, for his young readers and for those lucky enough to have not yet fully joined the ranks of the blind herd of grown-ups, he becomes one of those intimate friends whose wisdom— as fragile as it is profound—calls at once for both our attention and our protection."
> **Robert Kanters**,
> *La Gazette des lettres*

"The charming work [won't be read] without emotions [from adults]."
**Louis Parrot,**
*Les Lettres françaises*

"A parable for grown people in the guise of a simple story for children...it is a lovely story in itself which covers a poetic, yearning philosophy [...] Through its flights of fancy, the book will captivate children as well as any other fairy tale. The watercolors, in their radiant neatness, have the fragile and ethereal texture of air, stars, and flight."
**Beatrice Sherman,**
*The New York Times Book Review*

"Children will be touched by the beautiful story of the prince and the aviator, in its discreet and true emotion, in the drawings on almost every page that illustrate it in a very simple yet excellent style. In short, this adventure is a delightful apologue."

**Emyl Cadeau,**
*Temps présent*

"Within the text of this children's book which is simple and clear, yet also heavy with meaning, and rich in marvelous resonances, Antoine de Saint-Exupéry has successfully incorporated all the essential elements of his serene and steadfast morality, one of the most noble moralities that a man of our age has proposed to other men [...]."
**Thierry Maulnier**

"*The Little Prince* has the three essentials required by children's books. It is true in the most inward sense, it offers no explanations and it has a moral. But this particular moral attaches the book to the grown-up world rather than the nursery."
**Pamela Lyndon Travers,**
author of *Mary Poppins*

"A haunted pilgrim of the clouds, the stars, the shifting dunes, the moonlit valleys, [Saint-Exupéry] has met all the jokers, all the symbols of life. [...] He has been praised and celebrated. But in reality, he has never really returned from the planet of his rose. In his eyes, there were always the reflections of stars. One day, during the war, he left for a desert, a desert of water, and, this time, he would never return. He disappeared, like the little prince."
**Paul Bringuier,**
*ELLE*

"That is where Saint-Exupéry succeeded. The serious people who respond to the book's second drawing (the boa digesting an elephant) by saying, 'that is a hat' are perhaps not lost; they can correct themselves. They may receive a pardon and be spoken to, not of bridge, nor golf, nor politics, nor neckties—but of boa constrictors, virgin forests, and stars. But if they can carry on reading the book without feeling the soft urge to cry, if they take shelter from its infinitely tender humor, there is no more hope for them: they have lost that eternal part of themselves called childhood."
**Pierre Boutang,**
*Paroles nouvelles françaises*

**RIGHT** An advertisement for *The Little Prince* that appeared in *The New York Times* in April 1943, humorously showing how critics were unanimous...in their disagreement: some assert that the tale is a children's story, others believe it a book for adults. With philosophical wisdom, the advertisement concludes: "perhaps you'd better read it yourself".

# 4- The Little Prince Universe

# The Aviator

The aviator occupies a singular place *The Little Prince*: both as one of the story's two principal characters and its narrator. Without him and without his plane's breakdown that forced him to land in the desert, we would have never known the little prince existed. The aviator is also the only character that we never see; his only presence is in his narrative voice. We do not know what he looks like, because he is never drawn. He does not even draw his plane:"that would be much too complicated for me," he declares in Chapter 3, as though echoing the regrets that Saint-Exupéry sometimes expressed about having difficulty making accurate renderings.

We don't know much about the aviator, except that he gave up drawing when he was very young, disappointed by grown-ups' inability to understand that the hat he had set down on paper was not a hat, but an elephant that had been swallowed by a boa constrictor. This lack of recognition led him instead to learn to fly planes—perhaps no worse an outcome, for his career as a pilot has allowed both him and the reader to meet the little prince. It also allowed him to develop an eye for geography, which is a very useful skill for an aviator to have ("At a glance I can distinguish China from Arizona. If one gets lost in the night, such knowledge is valuable.").

The resemblance between the aviator/narrator and Saint-Exupéry is striking. Both are airplane pilots, both have crashed in the desert, both have taken pleasure from drawing without ever being fully satisfied with the result, and both have been disappointed by grown-ups. "I have lived a great deal among grown-ups. I have seen them intimately, close at hand. And that hasn't much improved my opinion of them,"

confesses the aviator. In an early draft of The Little Prince, Saint-Exupéry reinforced these similarities even more, writing, "I have also written books and been to war", though he would remove this sentence, which he must have found too autobiographical. And, just like Antoine de Saint-Exupéry at various moments in his existence, the narrator has suffered from solitude. "So I lived my life alone, without anyone that I could really talk to, until I had an accident with my plane in the Desert of Sahara, six years ago," explains the narrator in the book's second chapter.

Although this meeting is clearly important for the little prince, it is equally important for the aviator. Both characters find a friend in one another and are able to put an end to their respective loneliness. The little prince allows the narrator to rekindle his long-denied passion for drawing. The aviator sees the little prince as a reflection of himself, of the child he once was who had long since faded into the dark recesses of his mind. The little prince is another version of himself who sends him back to his own childhood. He revives memories of the narrator's home and the Christmases of his childhood. And, above all, unlike adults, the little prince still has some of that sensitivity which allows him to look into the heart of things and grasp the truth behind appearances. If the aviator had shown the little prince his drawing of the elephant swallowed by a boa constrictor when he was six-years-old, there is no doubt that the little prince would have understood what it was...

**PREVIOUS SPREAD** The little prince lounging beside a desert flower…

**OPPOSITE PAGE** Early drawing of the little prince and the aviator holding a hammer (1942)

# The Little Prince

The little prince is a mystery. He appears to the aviator out of nowhere, as if by magic, after his plane crashes right in the middle of the desert. "I jumped to my feet, completely thunderstruck," says the aviator. "I blinked my eyes hard. I looked carefully all around me. And I saw a most extraordinary small person, who stood there examining me with great seriousness." It is no surprise that the aviator's eyes were "fairly starting out of my head in astonishment." He doesn't know where the little prince has come from—later will he learn about the existence of his home planet, the asteroid B 612. Above all, he wonders, as does the reader, how this "little man" with the "odd little voice" could have arrived in such a hostile environment without seeming "to be straying uncertainly among the sands, nor to be fainting from fatigue or hunger or thirst or fear." All the while, the aviator, who is an experienced adventurer used to solitude, wonders whether he will survive with "scarcely enough drinking water to last a week."

For the little prince, it is the world of "grown-ups" and their lives that is a mystery. There are so many things to find out about that he never stops asking questions. And he won't give up without an answer from the aviator. Five times he asks the grown-up to draw him a sheep until his new friend obliges him in a manner of speaking. The little prince may be small but his curiosity is immense. He is "a virtuous being, gifted with an exceptional sensitivity," according to Delphine Lacroix and Virgil Tanase , authors of a study on Saint-Exupéry's story. He is "courageous, confident, sincere, relentless, clear-sighted and intelligent, curious, and intuitive."

In search of himself and in search of truth, he wants to know everything, understand everything, and learn everything. In a mixture of wisdom and ignorance, using his capacity for deduction and reasoning, the little prince alternates between silence and questioning, naivety and complexity. He turns to the people and things he comes across on his way to try and resolve life's mystery. "What is that object?" he asks the aviator when he sees his plane. "What does that mean—'admire'?" he asks the conceited man. "What are the orders?" he asks the lamplighter. But the answers he receives do not always satisfy him. They only make the people he comes across appear even stranger in his eyes. The sight of a sunset makes the little prince profess the kind of sweeping statements, tinted with melancholy and sometimes cryptic in nature, that you would more expect to hear from an adult than a child. "People have no imagination. They repeat whatever one says to them," he observes in Chapter 19. Several pages later, he makes the observation that, "Only the children know what they are looking for," to the railway switchman.

By the end of his initiatory stay on Earth, the little prince will have learned a lot. As will his friend the aviator and the reader, too. "The character... teaches us that every man should search for the kinds of truths that can't be found in textbooks for history, geography, reading, writing or arithmetic, but in the memories of childhood, at the heart of the immortal child who discovers the world and becomes aware of his or her potential, the creative child who knows how to read the invisible signs that exist beyond the visible ones," write Lacroix and Tanase. Of course, the mystery of the little prince will never be fully revealed. Still, just like the two characters, each one of us will leave with more truths and teachings, greater maturity than we had at the beginning of the story, and that is the essential thing. And as we well know, the essential is invisible to the eye...

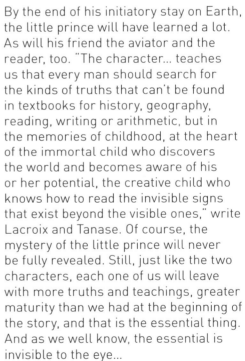

# The Fox

"It was then that the fox appeared." Opening with this succinct sentence, Chapter 21 introduces a key character to Saint-Exupéry's story. The fox is the heir to Reynard, the anthropomorphic red fox who has left its trace on literature since the Middle Ages, most notably in the *Roman de Renart*. He is also a descendant of the fennec fox that Saint-Exupéry adopted during his stay in the desert in Cape Juby.

More than a companion who allows him to break out of his isolation on a planet on which he knows nothing, the fox plays a role as the little prince's initiator and spiritual guide. He teaches him words that will become essential and impart meaning to a friendship: "tame" and "rite". "If you tame me, we shall need each other. To me, you will be unique in the entire world. To you, I shall

be unique in all the world." Echoing the little prince's own famous supplication to the aviator ("If you please—draw me a sheep!"), the fox asks, "Please—tame me!" The little prince will remember the lesson: "He was only a fox like a hundred thousand other foxes. But I have made him my friend, and now he is unique in all the world."

The fox also teaches him the importance of rites: "They are what make one day different from all other days, one hour from other hours...If, for example, you come at four o'clock in the afternoon, then at three o'clock I shall begin to be happy... But if you come at just any time, I shall never know at what hour my heart is to be ready to greet you... One must observe the proper rites." When at last the time comes for them to go their separate ways,

he entrusts the little prince with his secret, offering him the most beautiful of life-lessons: he teaches him to see beyond appearances. "'Goodbye,' said the fox. 'And now here is my secret, a very simple secret. It is only with the heart that one can see rightly. What is essential is invisible to the eye.'"

# The Snake

Able to solve every single riddle, and conscious of the little prince's fragility on a planet that is not his own ("You move me to pity—you are so weak on this Earth made of granite"), the snake plays an important role by his side. Thanks to its poison, the snake helps the little prince shed his physical body, which is only a sort of shell, so that he can return to his home planet. As Lacroix and Tanase note, the little prince and the snake "are not 'friends' who might tame each other; they intuitively know each other thanks to a supernatural knowledge. Instead of sharing a secret, they share the enigma of life and death."

There are three snakes in *The Little Prince*. The first is a boa constrictor swallowing a feline, illustrated in the book *True Stories from Nature* that the narrator read when he was a child, and which he reproduces from memory.

Next, there is the boa that the narrator himself drew after reading this book. Unfortunately, grown-ups, who never understand anything, thought it was a hat. Poor grown-ups! What the narrator had drawn, in fact, was "a boa constrictor digesting an elephant." In the face of this lack of perception on the part of adults, and rather than wasting time explaining things over and over, he preferred to become an aviator instead.

Lastly, there is the snake that comes to meet the little prince when he arrives on Earth. It doesn't appear intimidating to the hero of the story, who sees in it "a funny animal...no thicker than a finger", whom he finds "not very powerful". But the snake explains that it can carry him very far, "farther than any ship could," and as it wraps himself around the little prince's ankle, explains, "Whomever I touch, I send back to the earth from whence he came". Luckily, the little prince doesn't come from the Earth, but from a star...

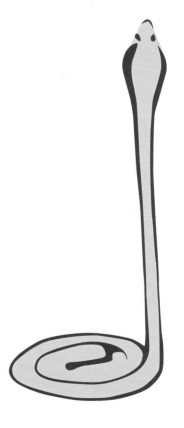

# The Rose

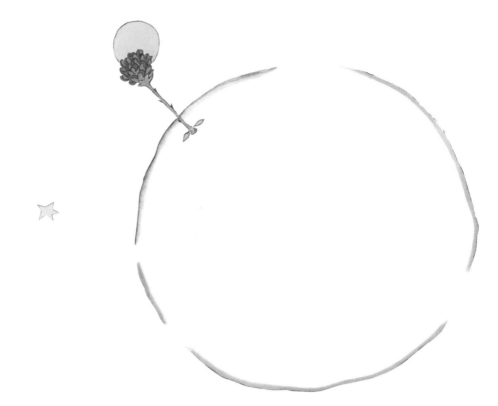

Without the rose, Antoine de Saint-Exupéry's story would never have existed. In fact, if it hadn't been for her, the little prince would never have come to Earth or met the narrator.

They had an instant affinity for one another—from the first morning he laid eyes on her and exclaimed, "Oh! How beautiful you are!" In truth, the rose is more than beautiful: she is moving. She knows how to show her tenderness and her "quiet sweetness". But she does not have an easy personality. She often complains and has a horror of drafts, which is hardly practical for a plant. Coquettish, proud, and self-assured to the point of vanity, with her willfully authoritarian temperament, she symbolizes the difficulties inherent to romantic relationships.

One day, tired of putting up with her remarks and tantrums, tired of feeling unjustified remorse and of the suffering she causes him, the little prince decides to leave his planet. "So the little prince, in spite of all the good will that was inseparable from his love, had soon come to doubt her," explains the narrator. "He had taken seriously words which were without importance, and it made him very unhappy".

His voyage to Earth, in the form of an apprenticeship, will allow him to measure the strength of his love. He will understand that his rose is unique and irreplaceable. He will realize the error that resulted from his youth and inexperience. "The fact is that I didn't know how to understand anything!" he reminisces nostalgically to the aviator.

"I ought to have judged by deeds and not by words. She cast her fragrance and her radiance over me. I ought never to have run away from her... I ought to have guessed all the affection that lay behind her poor little stratagems. Flowers are so inconsistent! But I was too young to know how to love her..." And his decision to leave Earth is motivated by his desire to be reunited with her, finally convinced how important the rose is to him by his conversation with the fox. "You become responsible, forever, for what you have tamed. You are responsible for your rose..."

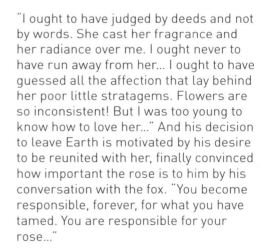

# The Sheep

# The Turkish Astronomer

"If you please—draw me a sheep!" Even people who have never opened *The Little Prince* know this enigmatic phrase from the book. Just as Saint-Exupéry is unable to draw certain illustrations the way he wants to, the aviator cannot meet his new friend's expectations. The sheep he draws is either too old, too sickly, or too much like a ram. He gets out of this tricky situation by drawing a box with the sheep inside. The reader cannot see the sheep but can imagine it, so long as they are able to see a reality beyond the immediately visible, like the little prince. But the sheep, which could decide to eat the little prince's rose at any moment, is a potential danger and must be supervised closely. So the aviator has the idea of muzzling it with a leather strap. Thus, Saint-Exupéry raises the topic of freedom and reminds us of the necessity of protecting those you love or what you tame. Even if that means sometimes restraining that freedom...

Like all astronomers, the Turkish astronomer is a very serious gentleman. But when he announces his discovery of the asteroid B 612 at an international congress, nobody takes him seriously because of his traditional attire. Luckily for him, everything changed when, one day, "a Turkish dictator made a law that his subjects, under pain of death, should change to European costume." At a new demonstration in 1920, "everybody accepted his report." This character constitutes the story's only historical reference: in 1920 Mustafa Kemal Atatürk was elected President of the Turkish Grand National Assembly, before establishing the Republic of Turkey three years later, and he banned wearing the fez, making the adoption of European clothing compulsory instead. The astronomer is the victim of prejudice at the hands of his colleagues from other, presumably Western, countries. They do not judge him on his talents, but because of his differences to them: their opinion of him changes as soon as he starts dressing like them. This character probably explains the popularity of *The Little Prince* in Turkey, where he is seen as a symbol of national identity.

# The King

This king is a strange king. Like all sovereigns, he likes to be obeyed by his subjects. The only problem is that he has no subjects by whom he can be obeyed: with the exception of one rat who sometimes wakes him at night, the king lives alone on asteroid B 325. He is reduced to commanding the sun and the stars. When the little prince visits him, he is over the moon. Finally, a subject to give orders to! He is a cunning king, because he is careful to decree only "reasonable" orders that can actually be carried out. He is also a philosopher who shows a certain wisdom. He explains to the little prince that it is more difficult to judge oneself than to judge others. But the way he wields his power is absurd: he suggests that the little prince become the Minister of Justice when there is no one to judge except the rat. "The grown-ups are very strange," concludes the little prince as he continues on his journey...

# The Conceited Man

On the asteroid B 326 there lives a curious character. He defines himself as "the handsomest, the best-dressed, the richest, and the most intelligent man" on the planet. He wears a hat, which he is ready to raise in salute to his admirers who come to sing his praises. Alas, nobody at all ever does so, or admires him: he lives alone on asteroid B 326. What a sad life is his! Amused, the little prince is happy to admire him if it pleases the man, although he does not know the meaning of the word. "The grown-ups are certainly very odd," is the little prince's concluding moral. The reader can be reassured that any resemblance to existing persons is, of course, purely coincidental. There is no danger that the reader might risk catching that strange illness called vanity...

# The Drunkard

# The Businessman

On planet B 327 a man is sitting by himself. However, he is not entirely by himself: bottles surround him. There are empty ones and there are full ones... that will soon be empty. What is the drunkard doing, with his red nose and his crooked hat? Well, he is drinking. He is drinking to forget that he is ashamed... of drinking. Don't you think there is something melancholy about it all? Indeed, this meeting plunges the little prince "into deep dejection" and into even deeper perplexity. He would very much like to help the drunkard, but he doesn't know how. In any case, this curious character won't be the one to reconcile him with the human race. "The grown-ups are certainly very, very odd," concludes the prince before continuing on to the next planet.

Like the astronomer, the businessman is a serious gentleman. In fact, when the little prince sets foot on planet B 328, the businessman keeps telling him that he is a serious man, "concerned with matters of consequence. I don't have time for balderdash!" He spends his days counting and re-counting the stars in the sky, those "little golden objects that set lazy men to idle dreaming." In the end, he puts them in the bank by writing the quantity he possesses down on paper. Quite rightly, the little prince thinks that this is not a matter of great consequence because the stars serve no purpose for the businessman, who cannot pluck them as he might pluck a flower and carry it around, or wear a scarf around his neck. And they have no need for the businessman. The little prince can look after a flower by watering it every day and he can look after his volcanoes by cleaning them out every week. "It is of some use to my volcanoes, and it is of some use to my flower, that I own them. But you are of no use to the stars..." he says to the businessman. This character, who was called "the owner," in a previous draft of the text, personifies Saint-Exupéry's inherent mistrust of commerce, money, and business.

# The Lamplighter

# The Geographer

This character is different to the others that the little prince has met so far. In accordance with his orders, he is responsible for lighting and putting out the single streetlamp on the miniscule planet B 329. It seems like an easy job. In reality, it is a nightmare: since the planet is turning more and more quickly, at a rate of one turn every thirty seconds, he no longer has a minute to himself. And the poor lamplighter, who so loves to sleep, is frustrated and exhausted. Some might find him absurd. The king, the conceited man, the drunkard, and the businessman would certainly have nothing but scorn for him. But not the little prince. "Perhaps that is because he is thinking of something else besides himself," and, "when he lights his streetlamp it is as if he brought one more star to life, or one flower." If only his planet had been a little larger, they could have been friends and the little prince could have watched 1440 sunsets every day...

Like Saint-Exupéry, the geographer writes books. He writes very wise geographical works in which he records the seas, rivers, towns, mountains, and deserts. But he does not know what he is talking about: as opposed to Saint-Exupéry who spent his life travelling the world, the geographer never leaves his desk. The geographer only compiles the observations and memories of explorers. He knows nothing about his own planet B 330 and has only a theoretical vision of life. But he takes himself very seriously, like the businessman. "The geographer is much too important to go loafing around," he says: he leaves that to the explorers. However, without the explorers he would be nothing. This character plays a decisive role in the little prince's life: he teaches him that his flower is ephemeral and encourages him to visit Earth.

# The Desert Flower

# The Echo

Having arrived on Earth, and after a brief exchange with the snake, the little prince heads off on his desert crossing. That's where he meets the flower, a flower with three petals, a flower of no account at all." He asks her where the men are. She does not know much about them. She believes there are "six or seven of them in existence." One day, several years ago, she saw them, "but one never knows where to find them. The wind blows them away. They have no roots, and that makes their lives very difficult." The dialogue ends there. Saint-Exupéry did not lack roots, on the contrary. However, that never stopped him leaving, like the other men the desert flower spoke of, on a journey of discovery across the desert and over the world. He went on this journey without ever renouncing his roots, the nostalgia-tinted memory of which will accompany him throughout his travels around the universe.

The inhabitants of planet Earth have no reason to envy the king, the conceited man, the drunkard, or the businessman: they are just as strange as they are in their own way! If you try and strike up a conversation with them, they will simply repeat back to you whatever you have just said. How can there be hope for having a discussion under such conditions? These people suffer from a terrible lack of imagination. In reality, the little prince is mistaken: he believes he has met humans but he has only been met by an echo, having scaled a "high mountain," and calling out, "be my friends. I am all alone." Used to his volcanoes "which came up to his knees," he thought he could see "the whole planet at one glance, and all the people" by climbing the mountain. In describing the scene, Antoine de Saint-Exupéry was perhaps thinking of those moments of solitude in the cabins of his planes, when he had no one but himself to talk to and could only hear the sound of his own voice coming back to him as an echo, just like the little prince perched on the summit of his mountain.

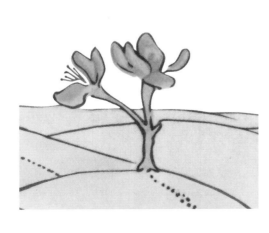

# The Roses

There are more surprises in store for the little prince on planet Earth. To this point, he had always believed his rose to be unique, but then he discovers a garden carpeted with thousands of flowers identical to his own—at least in appearance. "We are roses," they say to him in greeting. The little prince is overwhelmed with sadness, as though he has been pierced straight through the heart. His rose had told him she was the only one of her kind. "I thought I was rich, with a flower that was unique in all the world, and all I had was a common rose. A common rose, and three volcanoes that come up to my knees—and one of them perhaps extinct forever... That doesn't make me a very great prince..." thinks the little prince as he starts to cry.

Fortunately, the fox will soon teach him that the rose is unique in the world after all, which the little prince is quick to go tell these earthly flowers: "You are not at all like my rose. As yet you are nothing... You are beautiful, but you are empty," he says to them. He feels bad for thinking they were as important as her. "It's the time you have wasted for your rose that makes your rose so important," the fox explains to him. "You become responsible forever for what you have tamed. You are responsible for your rose..."

# The Railway Switchman

Every job has its purpose, and the railway switchman knows his: to operate railway switches. "I sort out travelers, in bundles of a thousand," he says to the little prince. "I send off the trains that carry them: now to the right, now to the left." We do not know when or where the little prince meets the railway switchman. We ignore that which all travelers are looking for, whom the little prince thinks are "in a great hurry". Nobody knows what they are looking for, not even the locomotive engineer. Men love to run around and get excited for no reason, even if it's absurd. It makes them feel alive; it gives their lives meaning, breaks up their routine, and stops them from getting bored. The railway switchman does not just operate railway switches: he also philosophizes. "No one is ever satisfied where he is," he professes. The only certainty, the little prince tells us, lies in children. They alone "know what they are looking for. They waste their time over a rag doll and it becomes very important to them; and if anybody takes it away from them, they cry..."

# The Hunter

# The Pill Merchant

You can recognize a hunter by his moustache, his gun on a strap, his red nose, and his hat. Whether or not he has ever been drawn by Saint-Exupéry, he does not come into contact with the little prince. Instead, the little prince only learns of the hunter from a conversation with the fox, who tells him how the hunter stops hunting every Thursday, a "wonderful" day, to dance with the village girls. This is useful for the fox, as he can therefore walk as far as the vineyards. "If the hunters danced at just any time, every day would be like every other day, and I should never have any vacation at all," he explains to the little prince.

One day, the little prince comes across a merchant who sold "pills that had been invented to quench thirst." You only need to swallow one pill a week, and you no longer need anything to drink. Here is an invention the little prince is interested in. He wonders what purpose it serves. The merchant—a businessman in his own right—replies that the pill saves 53 minutes a week. The experts say so, and everyone knows that we must listen to the experts! And what can you do with those 53 minutes? "Anything you like…" says the merchant. "As for me," the little prince says to himself, "if I had 53 minutes to spend as I liked, I should walk at my leisure toward a spring of fresh water." From the merchant's point of view, this little prince is certainly very irritating: he is not rational enough, not calculating enough, not productive enough. Just like Saint-Exupéry, perhaps…

# The Little Prince Environment: The Earth

Having visited six asteroids, the little prince discovers the planet Earth. He heads there on the geographer's advice, according to whom the planet "has a good reputation." Upon arrival, he has to admit he is a little disappointed. So this is it? This is the Earth? He was hoping to find some people, and so, "very much surprised not to see any people," he wonders if he hasn't got the wrong planet. But, if the narrator is to be believed, the Earth isn't just any old planet: one can count there 111 kings, 7,000 geographers, 900,000 businessmen, 7,500,000 drunkards, and 311,000,000 conceited men, not to mention the lamplighters. That gives us a total of "about 2,000,000,000 grown-ups". They only take a little bit of space: "All humanity could be piled up on a small Pacific islet," claims the narrator. But be careful! You cannot tell the grown-ups that, as they "imagine that they fill a great deal of space" and they "fancy themselves as important as the baobabs"...

# The Desert — The Star

The desert is the place where the little prince meets the aviator, who has had a plane accident in the middle of the Sahara. It is also the place where he meets the snake. It is a place of solitude: "It is a little lonely in the desert," muses the little prince. However, that does not stop a flower from growing there, because the desert is not without its beauty, as he says in Chapter 24 ("The desert is beautiful"). "Through the silence something throbs," remarks the narrator alongside him, similarly seduced by the silent vastness. Used to seeing the truth in things behind false appearances, the little prince is well aware that this apparently arid land contains its hidden treasures. "What makes the desert beautiful is that somewhere it hides a well..." he says to the aviator, who knows exactly what he means: "the house, the stars, the desert—what gives them their beauty is something that is invisible!" But without the little prince, without his laugh, his wide-eyed surprise, or his questions, the desert will never be the same again for the aviator. And it will forever remain "the loveliest and saddest landscape in the world."

Stars are scattered all across the pages of *The Little Prince*. There are stars on the king's ceremonial robes; the businessman owns stars; there are the stars that travel around in space and those that we spot above asteroid B 612. As the little prince explains to his friend the aviator, the stars exist for many different reasons. Some exist to guide travelers, others to arouse interest in scholars, some are simple lights for decorating the sky and inspiring poets.

But there is one star that has a particular importance for the little prince. One star unlike the others that Saint-Exupéry's character brings to the aviator's attention: the star the little prince will live on after his departure and which will sustain the connection between them, their friendship. This star is "right above the place where I came to Earth, a year ago..." he explains. Alas, the star is too small and too far away to show him it from Earth. "My star will just be one of the stars, for you. And so you will love to watch all the stars in the heavens... they will all be your friends," the little prince says to him in consolation.

# Asteroid B 612

Do not try to look for the little prince's planet on a map of the stars. First of all, it is so small you might not see it. What's more, it can only be found in Antoine de Saint-Exupéry's book. "The planet the little prince came from was scarcely any larger than a house!" the aviator tells us in Chapter 4. According to him, it is the asteroid B 612, which was only seen once through a telescope by a Turkish astronomer. And what is there to see on the tiny planet? Three volcanoes, one of which is extinct, and that is all. On one of the two active volcanoes, the little prince has set up a tripod to cook his food. And on the other he has put a funnel, perhaps intended to protect him from the smoke that comes out of it. There is not much to do on the planet. When he is not busy looking after it, the little prince watches sunsets. He loves sunsets. He just has to move his chair a little and he can watch several in a single day. Once, he even managed to see 44 of them! However, that day he was a little sad. Life on his planet was often full of melancholy. It is understandable why the little prince wanted to get out and see the universe...

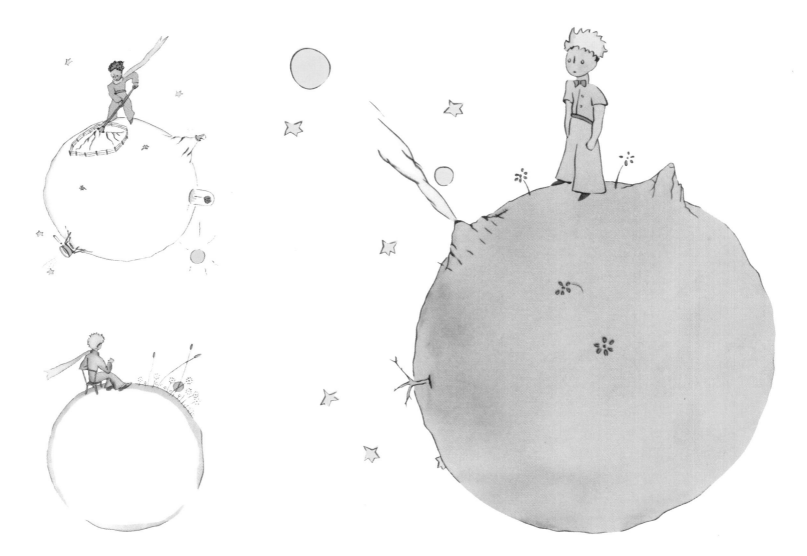

# The Baobabs

You cannot trust the baobabs, these trees "as big as castles" and with trunks so enormous you would think they are about to be inflated like balloons. It is not that they are naughty, not at all. But if you do not watch out for them, if you forget to pick up the baobab seeds that are scattered over the ground on the little prince's native planet, they might grow and grow until they make the planet explode. "It is a question of discipline," explains the little prince to his friend the aviator. "When you've finished your own toilet in the morning, then it is time to attend to the toilet of your planet, just so, with the greatest care. You must see to it that you pull up regularly all the baobabs, at the very first moment when they can be distinguished from the rosebushes which they resemble so closely in their earliest youth. It is very tedious work, but very easy." Certain commentators have seen a discreet allusion to the dangers of Nazism and the necessity of opposition to it in the story of the baobabs. The little prince's warning can also be read as a piece for advice given to the young readers—never put off until tomorrow what you can do today—and as a plea on Saint-Exupéry's part to protect the planet we are living on. This is the origin for the narrator's warning, "Children, watch out for the baobabs!"

# Objects

## THE TRAVEL MACHINE (FLYLEAF)

To get from place to place, all the little prince needs to do is attach himself by a thread tied to some birds flying overhead and let himself be carried away by them.

## THE PRINCE'S OUTFIT (CHAPTER 2)

The little prince cuts a fine figure in his outfit with his sword, as sketched by the aviator, although he has never seen this costume. "Here you may see the best portrait that, later, I was able to make of him," he confirms, still modest when talking about his drawings, just like Saint-Exupéry.

## THE SHEEP'S BOX (CHAPTER 2)

In this box that the aviator draws, there is a sheep... but only the little prince is able to see him: unlike "grown-ups" he is used to making out the reality hidden behind visible facades.

## THE LITTLE PRINCE'S CHAIR (CHAPTER 6)

The little prince loved to sit on his chair to watch the setting suns, his favorite pastime when he lived on his home planet.

## THE TURKISH ASTRONOMER'S TELESCOPE (CHAPTER 4)

Dressed in his traditional Turkish costume, the astronomer observes the

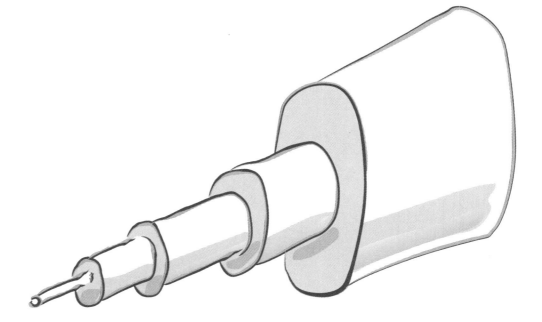

sky through a telescope that allows him to discover asteroid B 612. The size of the telescope leads us to believe that the asteroid is very, very far away from Earth.

## THE ASTRONOMER'S EASEL (CHAPTER 4)

It's on this easel, on which there are sheets of paper covered in equations, that the astronomer writes his demonstration proving the existence of the asteroid B 612.

## THE WATERING CAN, THE SCREEN, THE GLASS GLOBE (CHAPTER 8)

These three instruments allow the little prince to give the rose the care and love she needs.

## THE KING'S THRONE AND HIS ERMINE CLOAK (CHAPTER 20)

It's not easy being a king without any subjects, but one must retain one's pride all the same! The monarch keeps up appearances with his attributes of power, essential accessories for any self-respecting king.

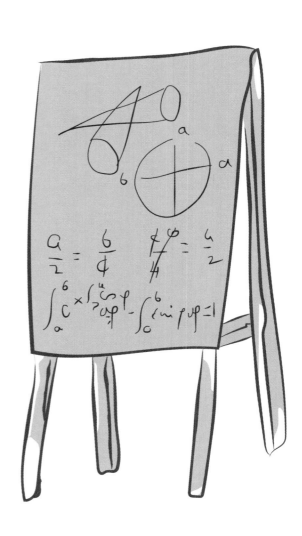

## THE CONCEITED MAN'S HAT (CHAPTER 10)

"That is a queer hat you are wearing," the little prince says to him. The conceited man uses his yellow headgear to stand out from the crowd and salute his admirers... although he doesn't have any, poor him!

## THE DRUNKARD'S BOTTLES (CHAPTER 12)

Three bottles on the table, six in a box by his feet: the tippler tipples to forget how ashamed he is of tippling. But he would do better, for the sake of his health, to forget drinking altogether.

## THE BUSINESSMAN'S CIGARETTE (CHAPTER 13)

The businessman is so busy counting the stars he owns that he has not even noticed his cigarette has gone out!

## THE STREET LAMP (CHAPTER 14)

To carry out his job, the lamplighter needs his street lamp. But this one seems different to other ones, as the little prince observes "When he lights his street lamp, it is as if he brought one more star to life, or one flower."

## THE GEOGRAPHER'S BIG BOOK AND HIS MAGNIFYING GLASS (CHAPTER 15)

This gentleman is without doubt a serious person: he has a strict demeanor and turns through the pages of his thick tome on geography in which he registers the mountains, rivers, and towns that the explorers have discovered.

## THE SPRING (CHAPTER 23)

The spring of fresh water does not exist in real life: it is simply imagined by the little prince during his conversation with the merchant who sells thirst-quenching pills.

*"SELF-DISCOVERY COMES WHEN A MAN MEASURES HIMSELF AGAINST AN OBJECT"*

## THE WELL (CHAPTER 25)

"What makes the desert beautiful is that somewhere it hides a well," says the little prince. The well he finds looks nothing like the Saharan wells hollowed out of the sand: it looks like a well from a village in the South of France. The little prince hoists up a bucket of water that is "indeed different from ordinary nourishment," that is "good for the heart, like a present."

## THE OLD WALL NEAR THE WELL (CHAPTER 26)

In the middle of the desert, a ruin of an old stone wall is as unexpected as a well. It is on this wall that the little prince stands up, ready to leave Earth behind, when the snake arrives at his feet.

#  The Little Prince **Quotations**

### THE AVIATOR/NARRATOR

"All grown-ups were once children—although few of them remember it."
(dedication to Léon Werth)

"I have lived a great deal among grown-ups. I have seen them intimately, close at hand. And that hasn't much improved my opinion of them." (CHAP. 1)

"When a mystery is too overpowering, one dare not disobey." (CHAP. 2)

"For I do not want any one to read my book carelessly." (CHAP. 4)

"Perhaps I am a little like the grown-ups. I have had to grow old." (CHAP. 4)

"It is such a secret place, the land of tears." (CHAP. 7)

"Men occupy a very small place upon the Earth... All humanity could be piled up on a small Pacific islet. The grown-ups, to be sure, will not believe you when you tell them that. They imagine that they fill a great deal of space. They fancy themselves as important as the baobabs." (CHAP. 17)

"In the moonlight I looked at his pale forehead, his closed eyes, his locks of hair that trembled in the wind, and I said to myself: "What I see here is nothing but a shell. What is most important is invisible . . ." (CHAP. 24)

"He fell as gently as a tree falls. There was not even any sound, because of the sand." (CHAP. 26)

"Here, then, is a great mystery. For you who also love the little prince, and for me, nothing in the universe can be the same if somewhere, we do not know where, a sheep that we never saw has—yes or no?—eaten a rose . . ." (CHAP. 27)

"Look up at the sky. Ask yourselves: is it yes or no? Has the sheep eaten the flower? And you will see how everything changes . . ." (CHAP. 27)

"And, if you should come upon this spot, please do not hurry on. Wait for a time, exactly under the star. Then, if a little man appears who laughs, who has golden hair and who refuses to answer questions, you will know who he is. If this should happen, please comfort me. Send me word that he has come back." (CHAP. 27)

### THE LITTLE PRINCE

"If you please—draw me a sheep!" (CHAP. 2)

"Straight ahead of him, nobody can go very far . . ." (CHAP. 3)

"When you've finished your own toilet in the morning, then it is time to attend to the toilet of your planet, just so, with the greatest care." (CHAP. 5)

"You know—one loves the sunset, when one is so sad . . ." (CHAP. 6)

"Be my friends. I am all alone." (CHAP. 19)

"What a queer planet! ...And the people have no imagination. They repeat whatever one says to them . . ." (CHAP. 19)

"I thought that I was rich, with a flower that was unique in all the world; and all I had was a common rose. A common rose, and three volcanoes that come up to my knees—and one of them perhaps extinct forever . . . That doesn't make me a very great prince . . . ." (CHAP. 20)

"Come and play with me, I am so unhappy." (CHAP. 21)

"I am looking for men. What does that mean—'tame'?" (CHAP. 21)

"I have friends to discover, and a great many things to understand." (CHAP. 21)

"Only the children know what they are looking for." (CHAP. 22)

"As for me, if I had fifty-three minutes to spend as I liked, I should walk at my leisure toward a spring of fresh water." (CHAP. 23)

"It is a good thing to have had a friend, even if one is about to die." (CHAP. 24)

"I shall look as if I were suffering. I shall look a little as if I were dying. It is like that." (CHAP. 26)

## THE ROSE
"I am not at all afraid of tigers, but I have a horror of drafts." (CHAP. 8)

"I have been silly, I ask your forgiveness. Try to be happy . . ." (CHAP. 9)

"Of course I love you, it is my fault that you have not known it all the while. That is of no importance. But you—you have been just as foolish as I." (CHAP. 9)

"Don't linger like this. You have decided to go away. Now go!" (CHAP. 9)

## THE KING (CHAP. 10)
"One must require from each one the duty which each one can perform. Accepted authority rests first of all on reason."

"It is much more difficult to judge oneself than to judge others. If you succeed in judging yourself rightly, then you are indeed a man of true wisdom."

## THE CONCEITED MAN (CHAP. 11)
"To admire means that you regard me as the handsomest, the best-dressed, the richest, and the most intelligent man on this planet."

## THE DRUNKARD (CHAP. 12)
I am drinking, so that I may forget, forget that I am ashamed, ashamed of drinking!"

## THE BUSINESSMAN (CHAP. 13)
"I own the stars, because nobody else before me ever thought of owning them."

## LAMPLIGHTER (CHAP. 14)
"There is nothing to understand; orders are orders."

## THE GEOGRAPHER (CHAP. 15)
"We do not record flowers, because they are ephemeral."

## THE SNAKE (CHAP. 17)
"It is also lonely among men."

"But I am more powerful than the finger of a king... I can carry you farther than any ship could take you."

"Whomever I touch, I send back to the earth from whence he came. But you are innocent and true, and you come from a star . . ."

## THE DESERT FLOWER
"Men? ...But one never knows where to find them. The wind blows them away. They have no roots, and that makes their life very difficult."

## THE ECHO
"I am all alone—all alone—all alone..." (CHAP. 19)

## THE FOX (CHAP. 21)
"One only understands the things that one tames. Men have no more time to understand anything. They buy things already made at the shops. But there is no shop anywhere where one can buy friendship, and so men have no friends any more. If you want a friend, tame me."

"Words are the source of misunderstandings."

"And now here is my secret, a very simple secret: It is only with the heart that one can see rightly; what is essential is invisible to the eye."

"It is the time you have wasted for your rose that makes your rose so important."

"You become responsible, forever, for what you have tamed."

## THE RAILWAY SWITCHMAN (CHAP. 22)
"No one is ever satisfied where he is."

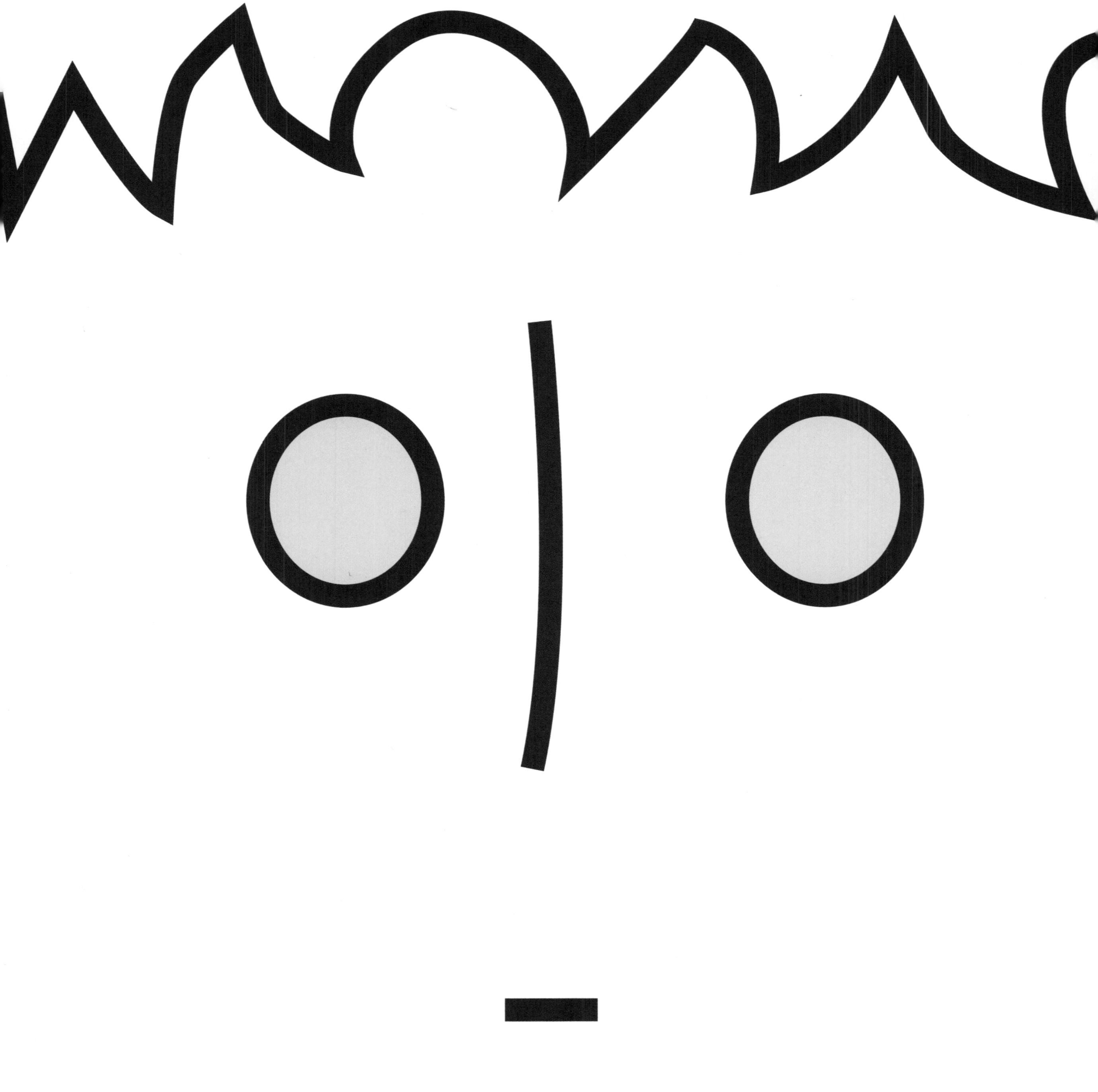

5- The Little Prince
Bookshelf

# Letters to Madame X

The letters remained the property of their recipient's family until they were revealed to the public in a 2007 Sotheby's auction. The following year, they were by Gallimard under the title *Lettres à l'inconnue* (*Letters to Madame X*) in facsimile with an accompanying transcription. They are testament to the importance of the little prince for Saint-Exupéry, but also to the role illustration played in the expression of his feelings.

Several letters included a sketch of his talismanic character. But the little character was not content with being restricted to just the margins of the text: sometimes the little prince is presented as the letter's signatory. It really feels as if it is not Saint-Exupéry who is writing the letters but, in fact, his alter ego on the page. The little prince played such a significant part in Saint-Exupéry's life that the author identified with him. In certain illustrations, the little prince's words and thoughts appear in speech-bubbles, like those used in comic books.

In 1943, Antoine de Saint-Exupéry left the United States to play an active role in the fight against Nazi Germany. He moved to North Africa and joined the French aerial reconnaissance squadron 2/33.

In May that year, on a train to Oran in Algeria, he met a 23-year-old female officer and ambulance driver for the Red Cross. He was smitten with her and began writing letters to her. But the young woman, who was married, did not reply to his advances, much to the writer's chagrin.

Some of Saint-Exupéry's letters evoke the platonic relationship that he would maintain with her during the last year of his life.

**PREVIOUS** The little prince, as drawn on the cover of *L'Énigme du Petit Prince* (*The Riddle of the Little Prince*).

**TOP LEFT** The opening illustration in *Lettres à l'inconnue*.

**LEFT** "She's never there when you call her… Nor has she ever returned in the evening… She does not telephone… I'm falling out with her!"

His words reflect their author's bitterness and frustration, dejected by his unrequited love and aggrieved not to receive a response to his solicitations. "She's never there when you call her… Nor has she ever returned in the evening … She does not telephone… I'm falling out with her! …I am reaching out to a friend who has forgotten me completely," says the little prince, who seems to have a look of annoyance. "I have made a melancholy discovery: my egotism is not as great as I thought, since I have given someone else the power to hurt me," writes Saint-Exupéry, who uses the word "melancholy" on several occasions and who refers to the text of The Little Prince in a tone that is, at times, particularly dark: "Look how I hurt myself on the rosebush when I was picking the rose… Nothing in life is important. (Not even life itself.) Farewell, rosebush."

"The author can no longer be distinguished from his character, his life can no longer be distinguished from his story as we know it, the world as it is can no longer be distinguished from the book we are presented with. This is Saint-Exupéry's 'true presence'; this is the charm of *The Little Prince*," writes Alban Cerisier in *La Belle Histoire du « Petit Prince »* (*The Beautiful Story of "The Little Prince"*, Gallimard). And so, "Saint-Ex" is the first person to provide a sequel to the story he published the previous year. These letters were acquired by the Musée des Lettres et Manuscrits in Paris, which owns a collection of original documents relating to the author. However, the identity of the unknown "Madame X" continues to elude us to this day…

# Sequels and Imitations

### THE RETURN OF THE YOUNG PRINCE (ALEJANDRO ROEMMERS)

Alejandro Roemmers is a businessman. But he is nothing like the businessman the little prince meets: he is also a writer. Heir to the largest pharmaceutical laboratory in Argentina, he has been writing since the age of sixteen. In nine days in 2000, he wrote a short book entitled The *Return of the Young Prince* (*El regreso del Joven Príncipe*). With a preface by Frédéric d'Agay, one of Saint-Exupéry's descendants, the work has been a real success and has sold tens of thousands of copies. Antoine de Saint-Exupéry has remained very popular with the inhabitants of Argentina, where he settled in 1929 to open new air route in South America.

In *The Return of the Young Prince*, the prince has grown a little: he is now a teenager. Having returned to our planet, he decides to land in Patagonia and heads off in search of his aviator friend. He will be saved from hunger by a lone traveler, in whose company he will set off on a formative journey during which he will learn the meaning of betrayal and dishonesty, ideas that had been perfectly foreign to him up until that point. Alejandro Roemmers claims that he did not set out to write a "sequel" to the adventures of the little prince. His story of initiation, intended for teens, aims to continue in the same spirit as the philosophical message offered in *The Little Prince*.

The author had to wait eight years to obtain the rights to publish his story in Argentina from Saint-Exupéry's descendants. However, Saint-Exupéry's fellow natives will have to wait until 2033 to read about the return of the young prince in the original language of the *Petit Prince*, when *The Little Prince* will enter the public domain in France...

### THE LITTLE PRINCE PUTS ON A TIE (BORJA VILASECA)

The little prince is very lucky: he has never had to work in an office to make a living. And, when he travels around, he does not have to contend with traffic jams and rush-hour delays on the subway: he just has to hitch himself to migrating wild birds. However, that does not mean the modern workforce cannot learn lessons from the little prince. That is at least how Borje Vilaseca feels: he had the idea of adapting the concept of *The Little Prince* to a modern corporate setting. With the subtitle *A tale of personal growth for getting back in touch with what really matters* (published by Opportun), the book tells the story of a certain Paul Prince, appointed director of HR in a failing company full of tyrannical bosses and demoralized employees. Paul Prince succeeds in restoring the workers' morale by applying the guidelines outlined in Saint-Exupéry's story. But the story does not mention if he ever drew a sheep on a flipchart or if he reduced the working week by fifty-three minutes thanks to some perfected little pills...

### THE RETURN OF THE LITTLE PRINCE (JEAN-PIERRE DAVIDTS)

At the end of The Little Prince, Antoine de Saint-Exupéry envisages a possible return for his character, and he writes "If a little man appears, who has golden hair and who refuses to answer questions, you will know who he is. If this should happen, please comfort me. Send me word that he has come back." Jean-Pierre Davidts grants this request. This storyteller and novelist, who was born in Belgium and lives in Quebec, published the book *Le Petit Prince retrouvé* (*The Return of the Little Prince*, published by Les Intouchables). A shipwrecked sailor writes a letter to Saint-Exupéry telling him that the little prince has returned. He met him on a desert island: the little prince was looking for a hunter who could get rid of a tiger who was threatening his sheep for him. Alas, nobody from the ecologist, to the ad executive, to the manager, to the statistician he talked to was able to help him. Unlike Alejandro Roemmers' book, *The Return of the Little Prince* was translated into almost 30 languages without the approval of Saint-Exupéry's descendants.

**El regreso del Joven Príncipe**

*Nueva edición ilustrada*
A. G. Roemmers

Planeta/Zenith

BORJA VILASECA

# LE PETIT PRINCE AU BUREAU

*L'esprit d'un grand classique
pour prendre conscience de l'essentiel*

**ABOVE LEFT** The cover of Alejandro Roemmer's book, which currently only a Spanish- or English-speaking audience can read, before it can be published in French… in 2033!

**ABOVE RIGHT** The little prince in office attire: a surprising image adorns the cover of *The Little Prince Puts on a Tie*.

# The Little Prince Archive

Il était une fois…
## Le Petit Prince

*Textes réunis et présentés par Alban Cerisier*

folio

## THE HISTORIAN

Alban Cerisier, an author specializing in the history of literature and publishing in France, has devoted several books to Antoine de Saint-Exupéry. *Il était une fois… "Le Petit Prince"* (*Once upon a time… "The Little Prince"*, ed. Gallimard) recounts the enchanting story of the tale itself. A compendium of texts, it weaves together critical contemporary reflections on the publication with current opinions. Cerisier retraces *The Little Prince*'s editorial history, from its different editions and translations, to its diverse adaptations. He paints a portrait of Léon Werth and takes an interest in the enchanting power that the The Little Prince held over James Dean and Orson Welles. The book also includes numerous testimonies from the author's close friends and colleagues, as well as writers' contemporary points of view of the work. With the sheer number of views it presents, *Once upon a time… "The Little Prince"* testifies to the richness of Saint-Exupéry's work.

**LEFT** The cover image for *Il était une fois… "Le Petit Prince"* uses a drawing entitled "The little prince and his rose" which Saint-Exupéry created for Lewis Galantière, the author's dedicated translator.

## THE ASTROPHYSICIST

Imagine... Just imagine that the little prince truly did exist: could he have lived as in Saint-Exupéry's tale? The simplest solution is to ask an expert. Yaël Nazé is a serious grown-up: she is an astrophysicist. Yet she also possesses a thorough knowledge of Saint-Exupéry's work. When she was little, she played the part of the little prince in a theater production. No matter what question you throw at her regarding the plausibility of the little prince's adventures, she has all the answers in her book, *La (Curieuse) Vérité sur le petit prince* (*The (curious) Truth about the Little Prince*). Available online, her book is a contribution that is as amusing as it is exciting.

First things first, do asteroids as small as the Little Prince's really exist? Of course, some can even be as small as a grain of sand. So, could the little prince actually have lived and stood upright on one? Yes, but the force of gravity means he would be wise not to jump. Instead, he would be better off walking really slowly and wearing shoes with grips so as not to float away. Could there be extra-terrestrial life out there? Astronomers are optimists; all the ingredients necessary for life (nitrogen, carbon, oxygen...) are found in the universe. Basically, if there is a planet, there may be life on it (biologists do not necessarily agree).

---

**ABOVE RIGHT** The Turkish astronomer, the only person to have seen the asteroid B612 through his telescope, is in some ways the ancestor of the astrophysicist Yael Nazé.

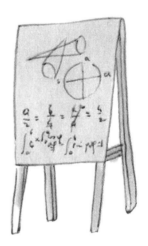

Could the Little Prince have smelled his rose's fragrance in space? According to Yaël Nazé, so long as there is an atmosphere, smells can exist. That said, it would be dangerous to uncover your nose and take a whiff of something on Mars, for example: atmospheric pressure is so weak that your spacesuit might explode!

Could the Little Prince have made use of the migration of the wild birds to get off his planet? Yes, given the tiny size of his planet, a single jump would be enough for him to fly away. As for the birds, they would have to watch out for the shower of little meteorites as well as ending up either burnt or frozen: the part of their body lit up by the Sun would be cooked and the other would experience sub-zero temperatures! And that is without even mentioning the difficulties of travelling between two planets, an interminable and boring process...

## THE THEOLOGIAN

Born in 1940, Eugen Drewermann is a German theologian, psychoanalyst, and priest who broke away from the Catholic Church. He lays out his reading of Saint-Exupéry's tale in his book *Discovering the Royal Child Within: a Spiritual Psychology of "The Little Prince"*, published in Germany in 1984 and translated into French in 1992 (ed. du Cerf). In it, he writes, "If so many people find pleasure in reading *The Little Prince*, it is undoubtedly because, with it's very visual language, the conclusion of the story seems to pick up the familiar religious belief in the immortality of the human person. But appearances are deceiving. Saint-Exupéry's starry heavens have only a metaphorical link with the heaven of believers. The Little Prince's departure doesn't promise immortality, just the chance to keep the dream of original man alive, and, in the middle of a human desert, never to betray our values, despite failures and despite mortality."

**RIGHT** When psychoanalysis lays the little prince out on the couch to explore beyond the appearance of classic interpretations of the work…

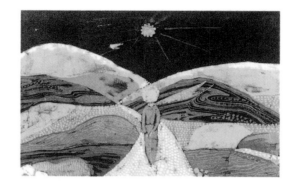

Eugen Drewermann

## L'essentiel est invisible

\*

Une lecture psychanalytique du Petit Prince

\*

*cerf*

## THE WRITER

Expert on Albert Camus and Antoine de Saint-Exupéry, university professor and Japanese writer Mino Hiroshi translated *The Little Prince* into his native language and has subsequently gone on to write a further two works on the tale.

In *The Enigma of "The Little Prince"*, Hiroshi analyses the narrative of the tale with an almost surgical precision. Paying meticulously close attention to each and every word from the opening dedication to Léon Werth down to the very last line, he teases out the possible meanings that might otherwise remain invisible to the reader's eye. Hiroshi also seeks to demonstrate that the apparent simplicity of the text in fact conceals a complex and rewarding system of thought.

In *The Encyclopedia of The Little Prince*, Hiroshi supplies Japanese fans of the story with information vital for a deeper understanding of the work. He analyses the conditions in which it was created, its characters, and the elements that make up the universe of *The Little Prince*, as well as the stages in the book's history and the different interpretations that have been proposed.

Just like Hayao Miyazaki, author of *My Neighbor Totoro*, Saint-Exupéry simultaneously succeeds at charming his youngest readers—who already know about the characters, the fox, the rose, and the snake, before even opening the book—and at prompting their older siblings to reflect upon the challenges of modern society. There is no doubt in Mino Hiroshi's mind that reading *The Little Prince*, a text he describes as "wondrous" is of great benefit for children.

---

**TOP LEFT** With *The Encyclopedia of the Little Prince*, Mino Hiroshi allows Japanese readers—who have some 20 translations of the tale available to them—to better understand *The Little Prince*.

**LEFT** Every sentence in *The Little Prince* may contain some hidden meaning, if we are to believe Mino Hiroshi, an expert on Saint-Exupéry.

# Books on the Animated Series

## FABRICE COLIN'S NOVELS FOR YOUTH

The Little Prince has a life outside the pages of Saint-Exupéry's book. Having returned to his beloved asteroid B 612, he lives peacefully alongside his rose and his friend, the fox.

One day, the snake tries to seduce the rose...and fails. He resolves to seek his revenge by extinguishing the planets in the galaxy one by one!

But the galaxy's in luck! The Little Prince uses his powers to prevent the snake wreaking real havoc. Blowing on his sketchbook, his fantastical creatures come to life. All he needs to do is place his hand on his heart and his starry costume and magic sword appear; in no time at all, he is ready to combat the Dark Thoughts. But will it be enough to defeat the snake? With fantasy fiction novels, radio plays, and comic books already under his belt, Fabrice Colin takes Saint-Exupéry's protagonist and develops him in his stories aimed at children between eight and ten years old. They are an adaptation of the animated series released by France 3 television.

**ABOVE** The little prince and the fox discover a planet that appears to be under a terrible curse...

## KATHERINE QUENOT'S GRAPHIC NOVELS

With fantasy novels for adults, youth literature, and magical books about witches, vampires, and elves to her name, Katherine Quenot took *The Little Prince*-inspired television series and adapted it for picture books aimed at young children and published by Gallimard Jeunesse (the publishing house's children's division).

## THE LITTLE PRINCE'S BIG BOOK OF GAMES

Will the Little Prince successfully dodge the traps that the snake has set across different planets? Readers must take up the challenge and see for themselves! They will have to triumph over the Dark Thoughts with a little help from the fox and the little prince's magic powers. From labyrinths to puzzles, hazards abound... But imagination and creativity always win in the end!

## THE PRESS: *LE PETIT PRINCE/ DER KLEINE PRINZ*

The French (published by Milan Press) and German (published by Blue Ocean) versions of a creative activity magazine were inspired by the France 3 animated series.

**TOP LEFT** Katherine Quenot's updated incarnation of the little prince battles the crafty snake in order to save planets in danger.

**ABOVE** From reading to adventure in one small step! With this book of games, young readers step into the little prince's shoes and comes face to face with the fox...

**LEFT** Games, comics, articles, and quizzes... Experience the *Little Prince* universe in all sorts of ways, providing maximum fun for young readers.

# The Little Prince Testimonials

**PIERRE ASSOULINE (JOURNALIST, BIOGRAPHER, AND NOVELIST, BORN IN 1953)**

"The Little Prince is Tintin's younger brother. It is true that Tintin has taken me around the world, but the extraordinary little boy himself managed to capture the world in a lunar landscape... A fairytale hero imbued with a sense of logic. He has an everyday kind of genius but all the elements of his universe work together to make him extraordinary. He is touched by grace and has an innate sense of wonder. He never shies away from asking questions, daring to ask what I won't, even when I myself am burning with desire to know the answers. Thanks to him, *through* him, I've asked everyone everything. Any understanding of logic and common sense, I owe to him." (*Out of Sahara*, in *Il était une fois... "Le Petit Prince"*, by Alban Cerisier, ed. Gallimard, 2006)

**FRÉDÉRIC BEIGBEDER (WRITER, BORN IN 1965)**

"This tale could have been named *In Search of a Childhood Lost*. Saint-Exupéry's constant references to serious, reasonable "grown-ups" reveal the reality that the book was not written for children but for those who think they are no longer children. It is a pamphlet against adulthood and rational people, written with tender poetry, with simple wisdom (*Harry Potter*, go home!), with shrewd naivety, that actually hides some offbeat humor and overwhelming melancholy." (*Dernier inventaire avant liquidation*, ed. Grasset, 2001)

**PHILIPPE DELERM (WRITER, BORN IN 1950)**

"The tone of *The Little Prince* is not 'Please—draw me a sheep!' nor even 'The essential is invisible to the eye.' The tone of *The Little Prince* is found neither in its story nor its moral. It is everything else: the sentences that begin, 'So I lived my life alone,' sentences such as 'I have had to grow old,' or even 'I shall cry'. The narrator of this tale is an aviator who no longer has a plane. The desert is all around him. When he comes across someone else, it cannot be anything but an illusion. This illusion is, of course, the spirit of childhood, forever buried in the sand or having floated away into sky." (Special edition of the monthly magazine *Lire, Le Petit Prince 60 ans après*, 2006) "For me, the book does not express values, but a poetic mystery which can be sensed from the first words: "So I lived my life alone..." Some people hate it, because it affirms the superiority of the childhood spirit over the mental universe of adults. But for some reason, I felt a peculiar resonance with this attitude. It is an astonishing book and, depending on the reader's age, preoccupations, and relationship with the world around them, it offers a different reading." (Interview in *L'Express*, 2011)

**MARIE DESPLECHIN (WRITER, BORN IN 1959)**

"Today, my view of *The Little Prince* is one of a great, wonderful book: sincere, bold, an instant of grace. But I also find that it doesn't deal all that much with childhood. The prince may be little, but he is no child, neither boy nor girl. He is just a soul. Of course, everyone can read a book about a soul. Even children. But don't say that this book is written for them, or that it resembles them. *White Fang* is not a book for dogs; *Moby Dick* is not a book for whales. *The Little Prince* is not a book for children." (Special edition of the monthly magazine *Lire, Le Petit Prince 60 ans après*, 2006)

**BERNARD GIRAUDEAU (ACTOR AND WRITER, 1947-2010)**

"I had met the little boy with golden hair in a totally unexpected manner, his way, your way. I was no longer a child, and I think I was at sea, somewhere off the coast of the Sunda Islands... I was dazzled by the simplicity of the tale and then, as I grew older, I cherished its depth, its clarity, its strength, and its joy, too. I'm always surprised that we consider it a work for young readers. I know that you wrote it for such an audience but, as a child, I would have cried when the snake bit your little companion and that he, when leaving you, would leave you empty inside. I would have cried when the little prince went away and my despair at the idea of never seeing him again would have been unbearable... "I have grown old, like grown-ups", but I tried to keep a bit of that little prince alive in me, and since I am a clever, sensible child, I have been able to understand you better."
(Special edition of the monthly magazine *Lire, Le Petit Prince 60 ans après*, 2006)

### ALBERT MEMMI (WRITER, BORN IN 1920)

"The Little Prince explored the planets; what was he searching for, if not what all wise men, all philosophies, all religions have also searched for is: how best to live life. What is the meaning of life? We have walked on the Moon and we will set foot on other planets; presumably, we will find nothing, not even water. We must bring order to our own planet, the only one up until now with an atmosphere that can sustain us."

(Special edition of the monthly magazine *Lire, Le Petit Prince 60 ans après*, 2006)

### DANIEL PICOULY (WRITER, BORN IN 1948)

Nowadays, the Little Prince would get himself run over by one of the Dakar 4x4s. He would have spoiled their stupid competition. A word of advice, little prince from down here: keep well hidden. Don't let yourself be deceived by the poetic mirage of the caravans. By the chrome flashes of their civilization. I wouldn't want to see you heartbroken on the road because the desert fox you were protecting has escaped from your arms."

(Special edition of the monthly magazine *Lire, Le Petit Prince 60 ans après*, 2006)

### PATRICK POIVRE D'ARVOR (JOURNALIST AND WRITER, BORN IN 1947)

"We owe such a great to deal to our legendary aviator. He was a kind of father to us all; to me, he was even a sort of godfather. I was so proud of my aviator grandfather (he had often traversed the same route as Saint-Ex, and my grandmother had a lot of connections with his wife, Consuelo) that, one day during recess, I told people I was Antoine de Saint-Exupéry's godson! That knocked the wind out of my little classmates' sails... and, from that moment onward, I was revered among them..."

(Special edition of the monthly magazine *Lire, Le Petit Prince 60 ans après*, 2006)

6- The Little Prince On Screen

# Cinema

### MALENKIY PRINTS

In 1967, Lithuanian filmmaker Arūnas Žebriūnas (1931-2013) became the first to adapt *The Little Prince* for the silver screen, just one year after the book appeared in translation in his native Lithuanian. Titled *Malenkiy prints*, the film retold Saint-Exupéry's tale with a poetic elegance and minimalistic charm. Žebriūnas's little prince was dressed in white with a matching scarf wrapped around his neck; the result was a look that simultaneously conveyed a cheekiness and naivety.

A number of scenes can be found online, for instance, the little prince's encounter with the lamplighter which is available on *The Little Prince* official website. A YouTube search will bring you videos of the little prince standing before the roses in the desert, dancing in time with the flowers as they sway in the wind.

### STANLEY DONEN'S
### *THE LITTLE PRINCE*

Stanley Donen had already enjoyed great success directing musical comedies (*On the Town*, *Singing in the Rain*) and thrillers (*Charade*, with Audrey Hepburn and Cary Grant) when, in 1974, he decided to take on Saint-Exupéry's tale. Richard Kiley played the aviator, broken down during a test flight from Paris to India. Steven Warner, a blond haired eight year-old boy, was cast as the little prince; producer and choreographer Bob Fosse (*Cabaret*, *All That Jazz*), the snake; and Gene Wilder (*Charlie and the Chocolate Factory*, *Young Frankenstein*), the fox.

Donen's *The Little Prince* strikes a balance between faithful adaptation, retelling with scenes added in, and musical comedy. Singing and dancing replace classic dialogue in multiple scenes, including when the aviator-to-be presents his drawing of a boa constrictor digesting an elephant to grown-ups who fail to understand it and who all exclaim, "That is a hat!" Some new characters make an appearance —the general, for example—while the geographer becomes a historian. Partly filmed in the desert in Tunisia, it contains some classic movie moments.

Take, for example, the scene in which Gene Wilder prances around as the fox, dancing the tango with the little prince; the scene serves as confirmation of his comic talent.

Yet there can be no doubt that Bob Fosse's *Snake in the Grass* dance (which he also choreographed) is the film's standout performance. More than that, the actor-dancer's performance very evidently influenced the choreography in the music video for Michael Jackson's 1982 hit *Billie Jean*. From the clothes (black outfit, black hat, white gaiters) to the way he moves his body, from the way he spins on the spot to how he moves his hands, from the way he balances himself on his tiptoes to the famous "moonwalk", Michael Jackson was paying homage to Bob Fosse's dance moves, to say the very least. Could it be that the "King of Pop", who named his youngest son Prince Michael, was pop music's little prince?

**PREVIOUS PAGES** The little prince as he appears in Mark Osborne's animated film.

**OPPOSITE PAGE** the reptile wrapped around the branch soon transforms into a human and performs a dance routine in honor of the little prince. A certain Michael Jackson will later take inspiration from the scene…

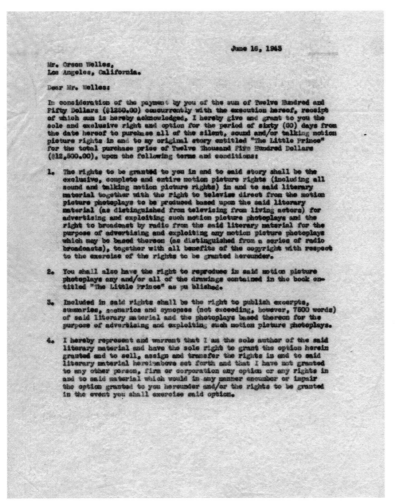

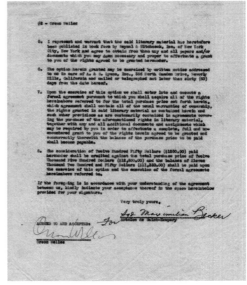

## ORSON WELLES' PLANS FOR ADAPTATION

Orson Welles had dreamed of adapting *Wind, Sand and Stars* and, when a similar enthusiasm for *The Little Prince* took hold of him, his passion was such that he awoke in the middle of the night to tell his associate his plans. Saint-Exupéry, too, never hesitated to call his friends, no matter what time of day or night it was, to solicit their thoughts on his prose... Welles envisaged a film with a star-studded cast, complete with animated sequences relating the Little Prince's travels to different planets. He sought collaboration with Walt Disney—who was far from keen—before renouncing his plans on account of Disney's refusal.

"There is no room on this lot for two geniuses," Disney would tell one of his collaborators, as an explanation for his decision...

From the four copies of the script, now stored in the archives at Bloomington (Indiana) University, it seems that Orson Welles wanted to respect the feel and spirit of *The Little Prince* and had reserved the role of narrator and aviator for himself. There is nothing surprising about Welles' infatuation, and we can see clear nods to Saint-Exupéry's tale in his 1940 film *Citizen Kane*. Both deal with themes such as nostalgia for childhood, the overbearing power of money, the menacing shadow of death, and the loss of innocence.

## JAMES DEAN, HOLLYWOOD'S LITTLE PRINCE

"Hello Mr. Wilder, it's the little prince..." If legend is to be to believed, this is how James Dean introduced himself to composer Alec Wilder, following his arrival in New York in 1951. Dean adored *The Little Prince*. He saw himself in the character, and shared the same mix of touching fragility and mischievousness. Dean even told one of his girlfriends that he had met Saint-Exupéry while the author was staying in New York in the early 1940s... when Dean was no more than a ten-year-old boy, still living with his uncle and aunt in Indiana! James Dean would never get the chance to realize his plans to adapt *The Little Prince*. In 1955, he was killed in a car accident, at the tender age of 24.

**RIGHT** Legendary actor James Dean was a fanatical reader of *The Little Prince*.

**BELOW** From left to right, Bernard Campan, Pascal Légitimus, and Didier Bourdon, the renowned French comedy trio *Les Inconnus*, are moved to tears reading Saint-Exupéry's tale in *The Three Brothers* (1995).

## THE THREE BROTHERS

Released in 1995, the film tells the story of three reunited brothers (played by the trio of French comics *Les Inconnus*) who did not previously know each other but who share various adventures accompanied by one of the brother's young son. In one scene, Didier Bourdon reads Chapter 21 of *The Little Prince* as a bedtime story to the boy, before breaking down into tears with his two siblings... Though no one has any desire to admit that it is Saint-Exupéry's tale that has them blubbering!

In 1990, Jean-Louis Guillermou directed an adaptation of *The Little Prince*, starring Guy Gravis, Daniel Royan, and Alexandre Warner. Though never shown in movie theaters, it was released on VHS cassette.

## MARK OSBORNE'S ANIMATED FEATURE

This film tells the tale of a little girl who is incredibly bright but incredibly bored, left alone at home during summer vacation. Her ambitious and workaholic mother has no time to look after her but instead sets out a rigorous study schedule that fills up the day, every day. On the first day of vacation, without any warning ,a propeller crashes through the wall and lands in the living room from the house next door. Her neighbor is a quirky old man, slightly eccentric but very kind, who is building an airplane in his garden among the flowers and butterflies. Next, a paper airplane flies in through the window and lands on her desk. On the folded paper, we see a drawing of a strange young boy and read the beginning of a wonderful story about a little prince who meets an aviator whose plane has broken down in the desert...

So marks the beginning of a beautiful friendship between the little girl and the old man, and she visits his house, an Ali Baba's cave of wonders. For the first time ever, the neighbor shares the story about the little man with golden hair. He tells her all about the little prince's adventures: life on his planet, his love for his rose, and his encounters with grown-ups, among many other things. The girl's mother becomes angry when she realizes that her daughter is off climbing trees instead of following the schedule she imposed to ensure her success as a grown-up. Worse still, she forbids her daughter from seeing the neighbor again.

---

**ABOVE** The visuals for the little prince and the fox were inspired by Saint-Exupéry's drawings.

**RIGHT** The king gains a scepter and his robes take on various colors.

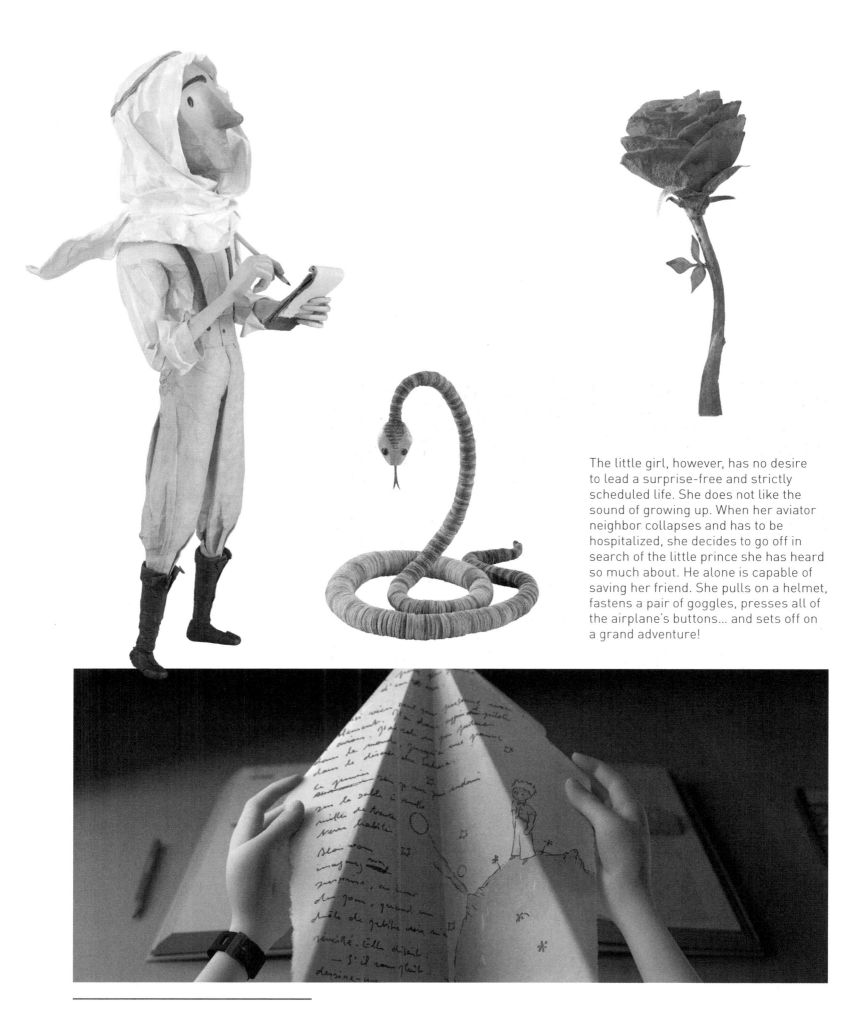

The little girl, however, has no desire to lead a surprise-free and strictly scheduled life. She does not like the sound of growing up. When her aviator neighbor collapses and has to be hospitalized, she decides to go off in search of the little prince she has heard so much about. He alone is capable of saving her friend. She pulls on a helmet, fastens a pair of goggles, presses all of the airplane's buttons... and sets off on a grand adventure!

**TOP** The aviator, the snake, and the rose as imagined by Mark Osborne and his team.

**ABOVE** An unusual paper airplane that tells the story of an aviator whose plane has broken down in the middle of the desert…

For the first time, Antoine de Saint-Exupéry's tale is the subject of a full-length animated feature film. Director Mark Osborne is no stranger to the screen, having worked with John Stevenson to produce the 2008 hit *Kung Fu Panda*, which tells the story of a clumsy giant panda who dreams of becoming a great master of martial arts. "I thought about it a lot and I realized that the key would be to tell a bigger story that encompassed the book. A story that would serve as a buffer for the little prince and his adventure," explained Mark Osborne regarding his concept for the adaption. Armed with a budget of $77.5 million, the director pulled out all the stops to get his vision for the tale across on screen. He mixed two animation techniques: 3D computer animation for scenes taking place in the real world and stop-motion animation for the universe of *The Little Prince*.

Mark Osborne was assisted by a team of seasoned professionals, including Bob Persichetti (*Tarzan*, *Shrek 2*) and production designer Lou Romano (*The Incredibles*, *Ratatouille*, *Monsters Inc.*). Peter de Sève (who produces cover designs for *The New Yorker*, and has worked on *Tarzan*, *Mulan*, *Ice Age*, and *Finding Nemo*) was in charge of creating the characters, Hidetaka Yosumi (*Tangled*, *Wreck-It Ralph*) worked on their expressions, Jason Boose (*Lilo and Stitch*, *Cars*, *Wall-E*) brought them to life through animation, and Alexander Juhasz used watercolors to design the backdrops for the stop-motion sequences. The soundtrack was entrusted to Hans Zimmer, eight-time Oscar winner for his original soundtracks, including *Gladiator*, *Inception*, *Kung Fu Panda*, and *The Lion King*.

**OPPOSITE PAGE, TOP LEFT** The conceited man stands atop his planet.

**OPPOSITE PAGE, MIDDLE LEFT** The businessman is swamped with work.

**OPPOSITE PAGE, BOTTOM** The narrator's plane lies silent in the desert dunes.

**TOP RIGHT** The academy teacher, the businessman, and the policeman: their appearances belie their natures.

**ABOVE** The rose garden in the little prince's universe.

In the English-language version of the film, the main characters' voices included actors Rachel McAdams (the mom), Jeff Bridges (the aviator), Albert Brooks (the businessman), James Franco (the fox), Ricky Gervais (the conceited man), and Benicio del Toro (the snake).

In the French version, they were dubbed by Clara Poincaré (the little girl), Florence Foresti (the mom), André Dussollier (the aviator), Vincent Cassel (the fox), Guillaume Gallienne (the snake), Vincent Lindon (the businessman), Laurent Lafitte (the conceited man), and Guillaume Canet (Mr. Prince). In both versions, French actress Marion Cotillard lends her voice to the rose. Attentive viewers are encouraged to notice the film's veiled reference to Léon Werth, Saint-Exupéry's friend to whom he dedicated *The Little Prince*...

# Television

## HOSHI NO OJISAMA PUCHI PURANSU

In 1978, *Hoshi no Ojisama Puchi Puransu* (*The Adventures of The Little Prince*) was broadcast on television in Japan as part of children's programming. It was a cartoon series composed of 39 episodes created by the Japanese studio Knack Productions, adapted for release in the US in 1982 and broadcast around the world three years later. The credits of the Western version carefully specified that the series was inspired by Antoine de Saint-Exupéry's hero, and "not directly by the book itself." Indeed, any reader well acquainted with the tale will find it hard to miss the extent of artistic license taken by the creators.

On his planet, B 612, the little prince sleeps in a comfortable bed which is sheltered by a wall with a tower on top, before getting up to cook an egg and heat his coffee over the planet's two volcanoes. Next, he does a bit of exercise by running after his friends the butterflies. His rose is a pretty young flower with a turned-up nose and eyes so big they resemble those of the manga hero, Candy. The general aesthetic bears a heavy stamp of Japanese animation's graphic preferences at that time. Swifty, a travelling bird with the appearance of a wizened old man, encourages the little prince to explore the other planets; and so he sets off to discover the great big universe, catching a ride first from flock of wild birds and then on the tail of a comet that he leaps and catches with his butterfly net... One amusing detail to note is the French expressions such as *n'est-ce pas?*, *voilà*, and *c'est bon!* sprinkled among the dialogues of the English-language version.

As with all adaptations taking artistic liberties with the original work, this version of *The Little Prince* may surprise and even annoy purists—yet, it is not always the purists' prerogative to be irritated once anything is done to "their" favorite universe? From the color palette used, to Dale Schacker's theme tune, the cast of vibrant characters, and the cheerful good humor that emanates from the production, the finished product is a series that makes for rather enjoyable watching. The Japanese pronunciation of "little prince" (*puchi puransu*) is just icing on the cake...

## THE LITTLE PRINCE IN CLAYMATION

In 1979, American Will Vinton, who pioneered stop-motion animation using modeling clay, employed the claymation technique to create a 28-minute short film adaptation of *The Little Prince*. Susan Shadburne adapted Saint-Exupéry's text and Cliff Robertson voiced the narrator. The viewer is transported on a dream-like journey through the film's quasi-psychedelic scenes, such as the little prince and the fox's first meeting. All of a sudden,

**ABOVE** In Will Vinton's version of the tale, the rose transforms into a young girl while dancing with the Little Prince before returning into her original form.

their blue and yellow silhouettes morph into a series of abstract shapes, which strike up a bizarre dance in celebration of their brand new friendship. There is a bluish light that bathes the entire film, while the snake is presented like a phantom; its body is but a beam of yellow light that reverberates as he moves and Vincent Price, who voiced the creature, sets a sinister tone. Meanwhile, a bushy mustache grows on the aviator's face that drags under

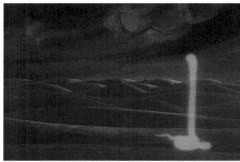

**THIS PAGE** Will Vinton's aminated short reflects Saint-Exupéry's poetic imagination.

his feet as he walks through the sand, his movements no doubt limited by the constraints of technology at the time. The rose is graceful and coquettish as can be and appears to be fixing her hair before transforming into a young girl and beginning a dance with the Little Prince. It is a unique adaption, full of outdated charm, and worthy of being rediscovered.

## DER KLEINE PRINZ

In 1966, East German television broadcast a TV movie of *The Little Prince* (*Der Kleine Prinz*), directed by Konrad Wolf. Years later, in 1990, ZDF, West Germany's second public television channel, took a turn at re-imagining Saint-Exupéry's tale for television.

ZDF's TV adaption came in the form of an hour-long film produced by Theo Kerp. The animation was traditional, with watercolor backgrounds. The little prince sports a spiky hairdo that would not look out of place on manga character Naruto and wears a bizarre pair of high-waisted blue trousers. As for the aviator, his three-day (if not more) beard is a questionable artistic decision, covering half his face and leaving no gap around his mouth.

For all its occasional obsolete animation sequences, such as the scene where the two characters walk awkwardly through the desert, the film does not lack appeal. There is a certain poetry in the shot of the little prince sitting on a wooden chair on top of his blue planet, or in the frame of him sitting side-by-side with the fox in the grass, facing the sun. As for the businessman's planet, the huge numbers loosely piled on the ground like a heap of rocks make for a quirky sight.

There is one issue, however: the series is only available in its original-language version and so knowledge of German is mandatory. Not that it is entirely in German; French speakers may enjoy the scene where the little prince departs from his planet and, mounted on a dove, bids, "Adieu."

**THIS PAGE** The little prince with the aviator, the king, and the conceited man in Konrad Wolf's adaptation.

### RICHARD BOHRINGER

In 1990, esteemed French actor Richard Bohringer was cast as both the aviator and narrator in a television series of *The Little Prince* directed by Jean-Louis Cap, who had already directed numerous television productions. Bohringer, who holds a great affection for Africa, made an endearing and convincing aviator with his warm, husky voice, his vehemence, and modest personality. Florence Caillon provided the voiceover for the little prince.

### *LOST*

In the fifthe season of the American television series *Lost*, the fourth episode, entitled *The Little Prince*, explores the character of Aaron: a blond-haired, three year-old boy. The wreckage of a ship is discovered by the group of scientists bearing a mysterious inscription, "Besixdouze" (Bsixtwelve)...

### *FUTURAMA* AND *LES KASSOS*

The little prince once featured on *Futurama*, an animated television series mixing humor and science fiction by Matt Groening, better known for creating *The Simpsons*. The little prince is shown standing on his planet, waiting for his newspaper to be delivered, only for the said newspaper to fly into shot, smacking him in the face and sending him flying into space while he yells, "Horrible!"

He is also one of the heroes—or rather, anti-heroes—of the animated French series *Les Kassos* (diminutive of *cas sociaux* or "social cases"). First broadcast online in 2013, *Les Kassos* satires characters from films, comics, video games, and cartoons, who appear in a social worker's office to vent their troubles. The little prince, deliberately reworked and updated to fit a "trailer trash" image, does not have much in common with Saint-Exupéry's character; he is rude and impolite, asks the social worker to "draw him something" and mocks her because she "can't even draw *Naruto*."

**ABOVE** *Les Kassos* features a politically incorrect version of Saint-Exupéry's little prince.

## FRANCE 3'S ANIMATED SERIES

Characters in stories are lucky: they never grow old. Since his birth in 1943, the little prince has not aged a day. Real life is somewhat different, and humans are in a constant state of evolution.

Today's children have little in common with the generations before them, from their tastes to their cultural practices, their leisure activities to their favorite media. With reading no longer their primary means of accessing culture, books must compete with other means of expression and often find themselves left on the shelf. The magic of a pencil stroke on a sheet of paper has waned; it cannot match the persuasive force of a movie theater screen or a video game...

**ABOVE** *The Planet of the Amicopes*, one of the episodes in the animated series broadcast by France 3.

**LEFT** The fox becomes the little prince's ally and helps him to thwart the snake's plans.

With that in mind, how do you sow the desire in young generations to discover *The Little Prince*? Production agency Method Animation and its team felt a pull to Antoine de Saint-Exupéry's work, and dreamed of creating a "new" *Little Prince*. This took the form of a 3D animated series, directed by Pierre-Alain Chartier and first broadcast by France 3 in December 2010, within the its children's program *Ludo*.

The CGI little prince travels throughout the universe alongside his friend the fox, protecting the different planets from the snake's evil intentions and keeping the peace, as well as making sure to write a letter to his rose each day.

**ABOVE** In the second episode, the little prince continues to prove that sometimes to find the truth, one has to look past appearances.

**RIGHT** The little prince in his usual outfit, waiting to put on his cloak that makes him agile and speedy.

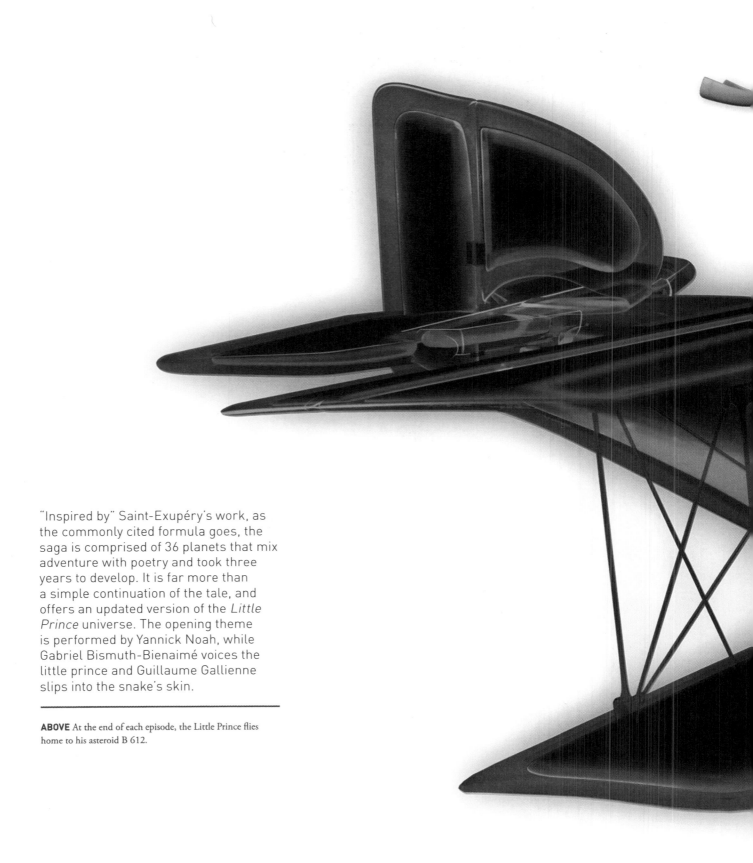

"Inspired by" Saint-Exupéry's work, as the commonly cited formula goes, the saga is comprised of 36 planets that mix adventure with poetry and took three years to develop. It is far more than a simple continuation of the tale, and offers an updated version of the *Little Prince* universe. The opening theme is performed by Yannick Noah, while Gabriel Bismuth-Bienaimé voices the little prince and Guillaume Gallienne slips into the snake's skin.

**ABOVE** At the end of each episode, the Little Prince flies home to his asteroid B 612.

# 7- The Little Prince On Stage

# Theater

*"SAINT-EXUPÉRY'S TEXT IS ALREADY A PIECE OF THEATER... THAT'S WHY THE LITTLE PRINCE IS SO AT HOME ON STAGE."*
*—VIRGIL TANASE*

Trying to draw up a record of all the times The Little Prince has hit the stage, even in France alone, would be almost as long and fastidious a task as counting the businessman's stars. In 1949, 76 rue Mouffetard in Paris saw the Compagnie Le Cheval arlequin stage "a two-man show with puppets and a magic lantern." In 1963, Belgian actor Raymond Gérôme took to the stage at the Théâtre des Mathurins in Paris for a four-month run of shows. He acted and recited a script while a color animation film, inspired by Saint-Exupéry's watercolors, was simultaneously projected behind him. In 1967, renowned actor Jean-Louis Barrault staged a eponymous show *Saint-Exupéry*, based on the writer's works, at the Théâtre de l'Odéon.

From 1977 to 2001, Jacques Ardouin's adaptation of *The Little Prince* ran for 23 years and over 10,000 performances at Paris's Théâtre du Lucernaire with acting from the Compagnie Guy Gravis. The adaptation was characterized by the simplicity of its staging and was performed by just three actors, two of whom played the roles of the aviator and the little prince, while the third brought all the remaining characters to life.

**PRECEDING PAGES** Saint-Exupéry's plane was recreated for a sound and light show at La Géode (an Omnimax theater) in Paris.

**THIS PAGE** The drunkard and the conceited man in the stage adaptation directed by Lorenz Christian Köhler, which was performed at the Admiralspalast Theater in Berlin in 2011.

In 1985, Bernard Jenny staged *The Little Prince* at the Choucrouterie theater in Strasbourg. Stéphane Pezerat wished to "become Saint-Exupéry's apostle, and present the magic, dreams, emotions, and philosophy of the masterpiece to an audience of all ages." Having staged it for a time among the dunes of the Moroccan desert, Jenny next brought it to French theaters and beaches, hoping to give natural settings pride of place since "*The Little Prince* can be appreciated to the fullest outside, under the stars." The Théâtre des Trois Hangars (located in Salon-de-Provence on the street named after... Saint-Exupéry) now known as Hangar Palace, has been hosting regular performances of Jean-Louis Kamoun's production of *The Little Prince* since 2008.

From November 24, 2011 to January 8, 2012, the Comédie-Française's Studio-Theater offered its own adaptation of *The Little Prince*. Directed by Aurélien Recoing, at that time in residence at the prestigious French theater, the cast consisted of four thespians: Benjamin Jungers (the little prince), Christian Gonon (the narrator, the echo, and the fox), Suliane Brahim (the rose, the three-petaled flower, and the echo), and Christian Blanc (all other characters).

In 2011, the Admiralspalast theater in Berlin staged *The Little Prince* with a woman, Nanda Ben Chaabane, in the title role, while Lorenz Christian Köhler doubled up his role as director by playing the aviator. The geographer was played by none other than Bruno Ganz, the renowned German actor who a few years earlier had played Antoine de Saint-Exupéry in *Saint-Ex*, a British film by Anand Tucker released in 1996.

**TOP RIGHT** Nanda Ben Chaabane as Saint-Exupéry's popular character. Why not the little prince played by a woman?

**ABOVE AND RIGHT** The conceited man, the aviator, and the vulture in the adaptation at the Admiralspalast in Berlin.

ABOVE In Virgil Tanase's production, young actors take turns at playing the roles of the little prince and the rose.

OPPOSITE The narrator is recognizable with his long white scarf and light-colored costume.

In 1998, Hurricane Mitch struck Honduras, leaving thousands of people dead and missing. In the wake of the disaster, Anaïs Barbeau-Lavalette, a film director from Quebec, spent a year in the country. *El Principito* was the fruit of her collaboration with a Honduran producer, an adaptation of *The Little Prince* performed by children from shantytowns. Having worked on the production for several months, *El Principito* hit the stage at the National Theater before being performed in Quebec in May 2000. In 2001, a documentary was made about these extraordinary little princes.

Romanian novelist, director, and playwright, Virgil Tanase is the author of a biography of Saint-Exupéry, published by Gallimard (Folio collection). Having translated *The Wisdom of the Sands* while living in Romania, he was no stranger to the writer's work and, in 2005, adapted and produced *The Little Prince*. It was first performed at the Comédie des Champs-Élysées in Paris, and then at the Théâtre Michel, the Théâtre du Temple, and the Pépinière, before touring France's provinces, and

then Dubai, Morocco, Switzerland, and Moscow. Tanase describes his show as "that of a guy who, when forced to confront the boy he once was, decides he must suppress his former self if he is to make it in adult life... That is, until he reaches that moment where we must all acknowledge that in our world full of deception, the only bastion of truth we have is that which lives in our inner child."

*The Little Prince* has appeared on stages around the world, in Germany as early as the 1950s, and from Italy, to Vietnam, and Africa. *Nabi-Bila*, a piece of street theater performed in Ouagadougou (capital of Burkina Faso) in 2014, brought the little prince into the 21st century. Having visited several planets, he wishes to return to his rose, but the machine he has been using to travel around breaks down in a street in Ouagadougou. While he searches for a way to repair it, the prince must face the city's inhabitants who are both curious and suspicious of him. He decides to tell them his story... Creating a play that pays homage to the inventive power of oral tradition.

# Opera and Musical Productions

Soviet Lev Knipper created an operatic version Saint-Exupéry's tale back in 1964. In 2003, English composer Rachel Portman did the same. Portman's *The Little Prince* consisted of two acts and 28 scenes, with the libretto written by Nicolas Wrightand directed by Francesca Zambello.

The work was developed on stage at the Houston Grand Opera and was performed at the New York City Opera two years later. A chorus of children served as the narrator and played the roles of the planets, stars, and birds, among other characters. In its first run, the rose was played by an adult soprano but was replaced by a young girl for the New York performances. Over 25,000 children showed up to the casting sessions and 6,500 children aged between 7 and 16 were called back for auditions... though only a lucky few garnered the roles of the little prince and the rose. A double CD and DVD were made of the 2004 performance broadcast by the British television channel BBC 2.

In 2006, German-Austrian pianist and composer Nikolaus Schapfl created a new two-part opera composed of 16 acts. Based on a libretto by Sebastian Weigle, it was performed in Karlsruhe, Germany. Schapfl's love affair with *The Little Prince* dates back to his childhood: when he was just six years old, his uncle gave him Saint-Exupéry's tale as a present. Nikolaus did not read French and could not understand a word of the story, but that did not stop him falling under the rose's spell... He began working on the project in 1990 and held the first audition for his opera in Salzburg 1998. The opera was

*"THE LITTLE PRINCE, AS A THEATRICAL MYTH, HOLDS AN ALMOST MOZART-ESQUE DIMENSION."*
*—MICHAEL LEVINAS*

to return to the stage again in 2006 in celebration of 60 years of *The Little Prince*, only this time it was performed at the Baden State Theater in Karlsruhe before an audience of 2,500. It was later translated into French.

Like Portman, Schapfl's aim was to create a work that would please children and families of all ages alike. His retelling of story features an authentic Lockheed P-38 Lightning on stage, identical to the plane Saint-Exupéry flew when he disappeared in 1944, and dating from the same era.

On May 29, 2010, the Mikhailovsky Theater in St. Petersburg, Russia welcomed to its stage a performance organized by the Offre la vie foundation with proceeds going to help sick children. About 30 Russian movie, theater, and rock stars performed some of the finest chapters of Saint-Exupéry's tale.

**ABOVE** Rachel Portman's *The Little Prince*, these actors among the lucky few to be chosen from 25,000 candidates.

**TOP LEFT** "Children, watch out for the baobabs!" cautions the narrator in *The Little Prince*.

**ABOVE** Could the little prince's singing be enough to help the narrator on his way?

**LEFT** "I believe that for his escape he took advantage of the migration of a flock of wild birds."

In 2014, Michael Levinas created an opera based on the work, which he put on at the Lausanne Opera in Switzerland. "The Little Prince, as a theatrical myth, holds an almost Mozart-esque dimension," says the French pianist and composer. "It simultaneously expresses wonder and grace, but also the supreme fragility and gravity that real, pitiable humanness must face: that is its paradoxical force."

From October 2002 to January 2003, the Casino de Paris was home to French singer and composer Richard Cocciante's musical adaptation of *The Little Prince*. Cocciante saw his work as a "pastel-colored musical poem" in which "tale mingles with music." The production featured Canadian singer and pianist Daniel Lavoie as the aviator and a young boy of 13 named Jeff as the little prince. Élisabeth Anaïs, who has worked with Catherine Lara, Garou, and

**ABOVE** The conceited man in Nikolaus Schapfl's opera, performed in Karlsruhe, Germany in 2006.

**ABOVE RIGHT** The snake, played by a woman, rises up behind the little prince in Nikolaus Schapfl's opera.

*"IT IS THE GATHERING PLACE OF ANGELS, THE CROSSROADS OF GRACE."*
*—ALBAN CERISIER*

Maurane, wrote the lyrics. Jean-Louis Martinoty directed and produced the performance. The production made use of special effects based on holograms and the costumes were designed by famed couturier Jean-Charles de Castelbajac. It was a huge success and toured as far as South Korea, a country where Saint-Exupéry's work has a veritable cult following.

In 2010, dancer and actress Sonia Petrovna dreamed up, directed, and performed a choreographed performance that she described as "metaphysical". Laurent Petitgirard composed the music and Éric Belaud arranged the choreography. Petrovna notably appeared in Luchino Visconti's film *Ludwig*. Supported by a cast of 12 dancers and about 20 singers, she brings a singular resonance to Saint-Exupéry's tale through her attention

to the musical ambiance, as she takes on the roles of several characters. "I love this text," she explained after her performance. "I find such beauty and depth to it... It contains all our humanity; it is poetry!"

From December 5, 2014 to January 11, 2015, Àngel Llàcer won the hearts of over 50,000 spectators in Barcelona with a musical adaptation written by Manu Guix interweaving ballads, jazz, and contemporary music.

*The Little Prince* has also been adapted for ballet productions in various countries, including the US, Canada, and Finland. In Germany, Gregor Seyffert directed a two-act performance that fused music by Satie, Pascal Comelade, Prokofiev, Bach, and... the French industrial percussion band Les Tambours du Bronx.

**ABOVE** The little prince and the aviator in front of the Gasteig Philharmonic Orchestra in Munich, conducted by Sebastian Weigle, on February 29, 2004.

# Multimedia Shows

In 1996, the French multimedia theme park Futuroscope released *Wings of Courage*, a 3D film directed by Jean-Jacques Annaud that retraces French aviator Henri Guillaumet's time in the Andes, during which Antoine de Saint-Exupéry makes an appearance. To celebrate the 25th anniversary of the theme park, whose 1987 opening was inspired by the new technologies of the time, a new sensorial attraction was shown in the aptly-named Pavillon de l'imaginaire (Pavilion of the Imaginary) to pay homage to *The Little Prince*. The universe from the tale unfolds in four dimensions: above and beyond the 3D effect obtained with 3D glasses, all of the visitors' senses are stimulated. It is as if they can feel the rain and fog, while blue lasers light up soap bubbles that float down among them.

On September 24, 2011, on the plaza at la Défense, Paris, a free sound and light display was put on by Joseph Couturier. The Grande Arche building was transformed into a desert for the occasion and acted as the grandiose setting for a reading of the story by actor Pierre Arditi. The little prince and his roses became enormous projections on the walls of the arch and the scenes of the book were punctuated by a superb fireworks display that played out before the spellbound eyes of the children... and their parents!

In the same year, at the New Victory Theater in New York, Rick Cummins and John Scoullar came up with a version of the story that involved just one actor, playing the aviator. The little prince and all the other characters were represented by puppets. Other productions have also used puppets: in Brazil, one of the countries where *The Little Prince* is most popular, the theater company Cia Mútua used them to tell the story of the author's life from the time he joined the Aéropostale to his death in *A Prince Called Saint-Exupéry*; in 2005, Richard Maska put on a spectacle of music and choreography that incorporated actors and puppets at the Ta Fantastika theater in Prague.

At the Sochi Winter Olympics that took place in Russia in February 2014, French figure skaters Nathalie Péchalat and Fabian Bourzat chose *The Little Prince* as the theme for their routine. By evoking the story, they explored the relationship between men and women, as symbolized by the connection that unites the little prince and his rose.

In 2014, 70 years after the disappearance of Antoine de Saint-Exupéry, the show *Night of Dreams* paid homage to him as part of the Fête des lumières festival of lights in his home town of Lyon. A product of the collective imagination of Clara Sigalevitch, Damien Fontaine, and Jean-Christophe

**ABOVE** A rose with a voice in full bloom in Futuroscope's attraction dedicated to *The Little Prince*.

Piffaut, this 17-minute-long visual extravaganza was shown once every half hour to its audience on the place Bellecour, the large square in the center of the city. In Paris, La Géode (an Omnimax theater) put on a show entitled *The Little Prince*, directed by Gianni Corvi and Pierre Goismier. This five-minute film retraced Saint-Exupéry's life using CGI, archive footage, and special effects, set to music by Verdi and Debussy. In the same year, in Nîmes in the south of France, the author's work was set to a dance routine by a troupe of 40 French, Russian, and Ukrainian dancers at the Festival d'été des Marguerites.

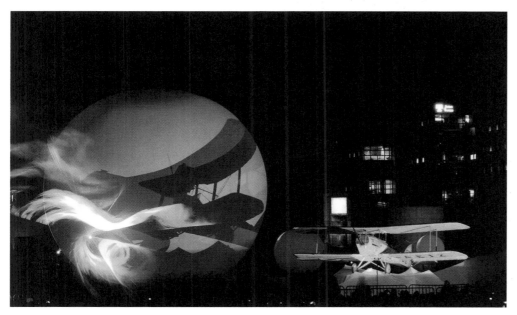

**THIS PAGE** Light shows and fireworks: had he been flying over the Grande Arche at la Défense rather than the desert, the aviator surely would not have lost his way…

# Audio Recordings

**ABOVE** The actor Gérard Philipe made a touching impression with his unforgettable interpretation of the narrator.

**ABOVE RIGHT** The sleeve of Reine Lorin's 45 EP of two extracts from *The Little Prince*.

Every reader of *The Little Prince* imagines his or her own incarnation of the sound of the little prince's voice, while reading and rereading the story. But without any doubt, in France it is the version recorded in 1954 on the 10th anniversary of "Saint-Ex's" disappearance, that largely contributed to giving the story's characters their lasting voices. In the role of the narrator, Gérard Philipe's warm and reassuring voice is complemented by the little prince as voiced by 14 year-old Georges Poujouly, who first achieved recognition alongside Brigitte Fossey in René Clément's 1951 film *Forbidden Games*. They are accompanied by renowned actors such as Pierre Larquey (the lamplighter), Michel Roux (the snake), Jacques Grello (the fox), and Sylvie Pelayo (the rose and the other characters). This recording by producer André Sallée was awarded the grand prix de l'Académie du disque, and is made up of a succession of extracts that lasts no longer than 30 minutes and makes up only a third of the original story but was enough to secure its legendary status.

*"I OFTEN REREAD THE LITTLE PRINCE : THE STORY OF THE ROSE AND THE FOX, THE LITTLE PRINCE MEETING DEATH; [THEY] FILL ME WITH ADMIRATION AND ARE ALMOST UNBEARABLY MOVING."*

*—GÉRARD PHILIPE*

In 1959, an adaptation was made for phonograph in Germany with Will Quadflieg. In France, Reine Lorin read two extracts from the story, *The Little Prince and the Rose* and *The Little Prince and the Fox*, on a 45-rpm record. But it would be 20 years before another French actor, Jean-Louis Trintignant, dared attempt the role played so well by Gérard Philipe, when he read the part of the narrator alongside Éric Damain as the little prince in 1972. The following year, the baton was passed to Mouloudji and Éric Rémy, alongside Claude Piéplu (the fox), Jean Carmet (the lamplighter), Danièle Lebrun (the rose) and Romain Bouteille (the businessman). In 1978, Jacques Ardouin organized a recording with the most in vogue French actors of the era, namely Jean Marais, Marina Vlady, Jean Le Poulain, Jean-Claude Pascal, with Jean-Claude Millot in the title role.

Since then, other famous actors have given their voice to recorded versions of *The Little Prince*, from Pierre Arditi to Bernard Giraudeau and Sami Frey (in an adaptation of *The Little Prince* on CD-ROM), and from several famous English-speaking actors such as Richard Gere, Kenneth Branagh, and Viggo Mortensen; to the German version by Ulrich Mühe, the unforgettable star of the film *The Lives of Others*. Lest we forget a digital version broadcast in 2001 on Radio Canada with Michel Dumont as the narrator and Martin Pensa in the role of the little prince.

**ABOVE** Ulrich Mühe's reading of *The Little Prince* is one of the most popular versions of the story.

_Favorites quotes from a masterpiece_

We write
of eternal things.

**To forget a friend is sad.
Not every one has had a friend.**

If you please,
draw me a sheep!

The thing that is important
is the thing that is not seen...

**All grown-ups were children first.**
(But few of them remember it.)

But if you tame me, it will be as if the sun came
to shine on my life. I shall know the sound
of a step that will be different from all the others.

## Children should always show great forbearance toward grown-up people.

...and at night I love to listen to the stars.
It is like five hundred million little bells...

Once upon a time there was
a little prince who lived on a planet
that was scarcely any bigger than himself,
and who had need of a sheep...

## The Earth is not just an ordinary planet!

One must require from each one
the duty which each one can perform...

# 8- The Little Prince in Comics and Youth Literature

# Saint-Exupéry: the Final Flight

"Hey, Antoine... Have you come here to watch the sunsets?"
"What are you still doing here?"
"If you please—draw me a sheep."
"I drew you one last time..."
"The other one went off with a star..."
"What do you mean it went off with a star? I never wrote that..."

*"I ALWAYS TELL THE TRUTH AS IF IT WERE FALSE."*

Monday, July 31, 1944, at 11:54 AM— as he sets off on his final flight before disappearing into the Mediterranean, Antoine de Saint-Exupéry has one last conversation with the little prince. The little prince is sitting in a chair on a cloud. At least, that is how Hugo Pratt, the creator of *Corto Maltese*, tells the story in *Le Dernier Vol* (*The Final Flight*). Hugo Pratt's stories should be read with great care, but not necessarily because they are figments of pure invention. "I always tell the truth as if it were false," declares the author in the introduction to his album. "Unlike many others who tell false stories as though they were true, I will tell you the reality as though it was made up. That's what makes it double, triple, and the reader then understands that some of the things I said were true and so it is with greater interest than before that they go off in search of those things."

Completed in 1994 (the 50th anniversary of Saint-Exupéry's disappearance) before being published the following year, this album was to be the illustrator's last. It is the fruit of a request made by "Saint-Ex's" descendants. According to Dominique Petitfaux, the author of a collection of interviews with Hugo Pratt entitled *De l'autre côté de Corto* (*The Other Side of Corto*), Pratt did not show a particular interest for the writer's œuvre and he would have been more inspired by Mermoz. He wanted to give the character of the little prince an important place, which was denied him on the grounds of copyright. So he imagined a story that oscillated between dreams and reality, in which Saint-Exupéry, moments before dying, relives the significant moments of his existence. The events of the flight are drawn in a blueish hue, while the flashbacks are illustrated with a sepia tint.

Because of a lack of oxygen due to a faulty supply line in his plane, Saint-Exupéry floats into a different state of consciousness. He passes clouds in the shape of sheep and meets significant characters form his life in a constant back and forth between the present and the past. "I feel drunk... Perhaps it's the American oxygen?" the pilot wonders as his senses slowly slip away. "It's getting darker and darker... It must be this oxygen... I should take off... this mask... I'm drunk!" Death comes at the end of the journey and the end of the album. First there is Saint-Exupéry's death, as he utters his mysterious last words: "I have found out what death is... death is..." But there is also Hugo Pratt's death. In the Autumn of 1994, just when he finished *The Final Flight*—a prophetic title—he contracted a form of cancer that would kill him some months later in August 1995.

# Joann Sfar's The Little Prince

## "I WANTED TO SHOW WHAT A COMIC BOOK CAN DO."

As a child, Joann Sfar listened to his grandfather reading him *The Little Prince*. He also liked Gérard Philipe's recording, and he was convinced Antoine de Saint-Exupéry had the same voice as the actor... "The book helped me understand what death is," said Sfar, whose mother died when he was just three years old. In an interview published in a special issue dedicated to Saint-Exupéry if the French weekly *Le Point*, the artist continued, "That's what the whole story is about: how to accept the disappearance of the people you love."

As an adult, the author of *The Rabbi's Cat* decided to tell the story in his own way, in comic book form. Why recreate an already illustrated text as a graphic novel? one might ask. "I tried to show that the comic book has nothing to do with an illustrated book," Sfar explains in defense of his decision. "An illustrated book takes form in intermittent leaps between text and illustrations. In the end, the graphic novel is closer to film in the sense that it only uses sequences. I purposefully changed almost none of the book's text. I really wanted to do that: to show what a comic book can do."

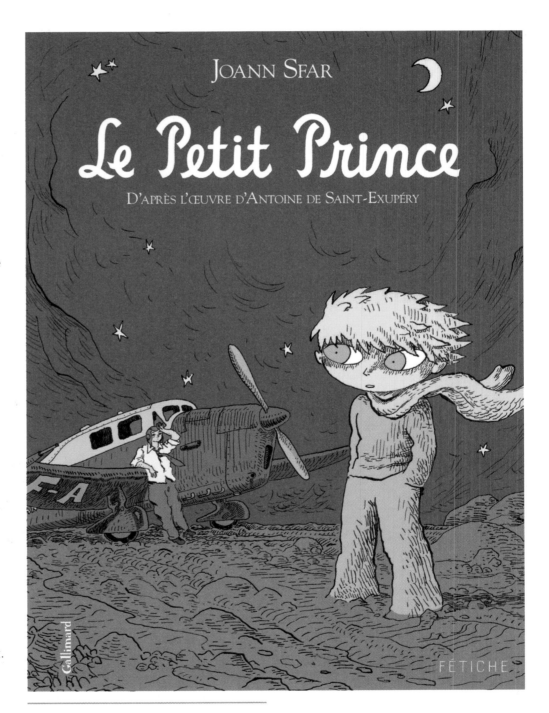

**ABOVE** Joann Sfar's interpretation of *The Little Prince* is a personal take that is still faithful to Saint-Exupéry's original.

In effect, Sfar chose to use the original text, even if he digresses from it at certain moments. Even though he stays true to the words of "Saint-Ex", his overflowing imagination makes it impossible for him to stop embellishing. And so, in the opening pages we see Saint-Exupéry alone in the cockpit of his broken-down airplane being lectured by his own cigarette smoke, which scolds, "You shouldn't be smoking in a story meant for children."

For Joann Sfar, there is nothing childish or naive about *The Little Prince*, which "deals exclusively with the essential." He also recalls that in Japan, Saint-Exupéry's book is targeted at adults: "Where fiction and religion meet in *The Little Prince*, there is a real spirituality: everyone is aware of it, and everyone has their own history with this great book."

He was reproached for having broken a taboo: depicting the character of the narrator—who never appears in illustration in the book—by making him look like Saint-Exupéry. "The comic book allows for an exterior point of view," is Sfar's analysis. "Drawing 'Saint-Ex' was a great joy. It let a morphological game play out between the little prince and the grown-up gentleman. When I was a child, I read the book and identified with the little prince. Later, when I rediscovered it, I realized that I identified with the aviator instead."

Jiro Taniguchi, the famous *mangaka*, paid homage to Sfar's little prince with big eyes: "I thought I knew this famous story but I was frequently surprised by Sfar's visual interpretation," says the author of *A Distant Neighborhood*. "This book brought me to a marvelous world beyond my imagination. It is fair to say that the story, which has survived decades, has just been reborn and that we have been given a new *Little Prince*." On September 15, 2008, at the L'Européen theater in Paris, Joann Sfar drew live illustrations during a reading of *The Little Prince* by actor François Morel.

**ABOVE** Joann Sfar's *The Little Prince* is available in color and in black and white.

# The Little Prince: New Adventures

Everything is going wrong in the universe! The stars are going out one by one, and the snake is the one behind it. The little prince decides to leave his asteroid B 612 to revive the extinguished planets. With his friend the fox, he will discover fascinating new worlds ruled by strange laws ranging from far-fetched to plain absurd. He resolves conflicts, combats ignorance, fights intolerance, and fosters communication between the people he meets. Will his gifts have the power to vanquish the snake and triumph over evil? Will he ever make it back to his rose?

Answers to these questions can be found in a series of 24 graphic novels, with each of the albums recounting the little prince and the fox's adventures on a different planet. Originally published in France by Glénat between 2011 and 2015, and by Lerner in the US, they are based on the France 3 cartoon TV series inspired by Saint-Exupéry's tale.

The creative roles of writing, scene division, artwork, colors, and backdrops are managed by different authors, all under the guidance of artistic director Didier Poli and editorial advisor Didier Convard (graphic novelist whose successes include *Le Triangle secret* and *Neige*). There is an added bonus to look out for at the end of the first 10 albums in the series: a drawing of the little prince by a leading graphic novelist. The artists invited to participate were Moebius, Tebo, Griffo, Matthieu Bonhomme, Pierre Makyo, Olivier Supiot, Jérôme Jouvray, Jacques Lamontagne, Adamov, and Keramidas.

**ABOVE** In Volume 1 of the series, the renowned cartoonist Mœbius sent the little prince and his friend the fox to a planet of angles that took the form of a giant cube.

## CHARACTERS

### THE LITTLE PRINCE

With his extraordinary powers, there is no one and nothing in the universe that the little prince cannot speak to—even animals and plants! When he blows on his sketchbook, the drawings on the pages come to life. Once he puts on his prince's robes, he becomes faster and more agile, and he can bring to life the creatures he has conjured up in his imagination alone by drawing them with his sword.

### THE FOX

Always complaining, always joking, always thinking about food... But, as the little prince's best friend, he is always there to come to his aid, open up the world to him, and help him grow up, too.

### THE SNAKE

Willing to do anything in order to plunge the universe into darkness, though its motives are unclear. The snake takes a passive role and needs only to bite its victims to bring out their evil side, which drives them to do its bidding and put the universe in danger.

### DARK THOUGHTS

Anyone bitten by the snake becomes a dark thought, once the serpent extinguishes their planet. Completely under the snake's command, dark thoughts act as a group and carry out its orders... that is, until the little prince stands in their way!

**THIS PAGE** A series which pays homage to adventure, imagination, and tolerance.

## THE ALBUMS

### THE PLANET OF WIND

Wind provides all the energy the Eolians need for warming their planet. But each day the winds grow weaker. Can the little prince and the fox save a planet from disappearing into darkness?

### THE PLANET OF THE FIREBIRD

According to the emerald-cutters, their planet devastated by fire is the work of the firebird. But sometimes to find the truth, one has to look past appearances...

### THE PLANET OF MUSIC

The voice of Euphonia the diva keeps all the lands in peace. But she has lost her strength to sing. What if it was love that caused her to change her tune?

### THE PLANET OF JADE

When a menacing mass of brambles threatens to invade their city, the Lithians are forced to evacuate. But the city's ruler awaits the return of his son Mica. Will the little prince and the fox be able to find him before it is too late?

### THE STAR SNATCHER'S PLANET

Someone called the Astronomer is uprooting stars and planets from the sky, to create a perfect replica of the night on his ceiling... causing serious problems for the Chlorophyllians' crops.

### THE PLANET OF THE NIGHT GLOBES

On planet Voltaine, people live in fear of the globes, creatures that are, in fact, harmless. The streetlamp seller is firing up the people's fear... to flood the city with his merchandise.

### THE PLANET OF THE OVERHEARERS

The Amicopes are a very talkative people, but flying machines, controlled by the tyrant Sahara, have taped their mouths shut! It seems that in this instance, sealed lips only fuel the conflict...

### THE PLANET OF THE TORTOISE DRIVER

Carapodes—wondrous giant tortoises—are in charge of delivering mail and resources to the lonely cities of their planet. That is, until the day when their guide, Arobase, walks out on them...

### THE PLANET OF THE GIANT

This planet is in the shape of a giant and functions like a living being, with each body part is managed by a different ruler. But, ever since Talamus stopped sending messages to the brain, the rest of the body has gone all out of whack...

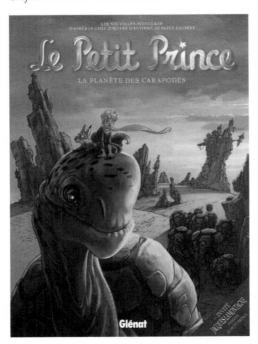

**ABOVE** The little prince will teach the inhabitants of planet Voltaine to overcome their fears and prejudices.

## THE PLANET OF TRAINIACS

With trains no longer running on time or getting to their final destination, life on the Planet of Trainiacs is topsy-turvy! Perhaps Hannibal, the railway switchman, has gone off the rails...?

## THE PLANET OF LIBRIS

Books have started flying away and disappearing! The planet has never had to deal with this before and, with all citizens suddenly prevented from reading, they do not like it one bit. Fortunately, the little prince is there to investigate...

## THE PLANET OF LUDOKAA

On this planet, two rival kingdoms decide to lay aside their habitual fighting over which one gets to watch the sunset and instead settle their differences over a game of Ludokaa. But the night before the big competition, the two communities are on the point of another battle...

LES NOUVELLES AVENTURES
D'APRÈS LE CHEF-D'ŒUVRE D'ANTOINE DE SAINT-EXUPÉRY

*Le Petit Prince*

LA PLANÈTE DES WAGONAUTES

Glénat

INVITÉ
KÉRAMIDAS
IMAGINE
LE PETIT PRINCE

**TOP LEFT AND LEFT** Two design sketches for the cover of *The Planet of Jade*.

**ABOVE** Accompanied by his friend the fox, the little prince discovers even more astonishing planets than Earth.

## THE PLANET OF TEAR-EATERS

On this planet, the emotions of the inhabitants nourish giant flowers—the Tear-Eaters—and, in return, their enormous petals protect the people from the rain of fire. But the Tear-Eaters are in danger...

## THE PLANET OF THE GRAND BUFFOON

This planet is in a sad state: the Grand Buffoon has sunk into a depression and has forbidden his people to laugh. Perhaps the prime minister, who dreams of seizing power, has something to do with it...

## THE PLANET OF THE GARGAND

When two childhood friends fall out over questions of power, you can bet the snake is lurking nearby... Fortunately, the little prince and the fox are there to stop him!

## THE PLANET OF GEHOM

The inhabitants of Gehom must walk endlessly to keep from falling off and tumbling into the stellar void! A handful among them have rejected this destiny...

## THE PLANET OF THE BUBBLE GOB

Bubble Gob, an underwater creature who is supposed to keep the ocean clean, is making something... But what? All it would take is one more tidal wave and the Creatalls' homes would be engulfed by a sea of garbage!

## THE PLANET OF TIME

In one village, time has stopped, while in the next, it is going very fast... Talk about befuddling the inhabitants! The hour has come for the Great Timekeeper to put time back on track.

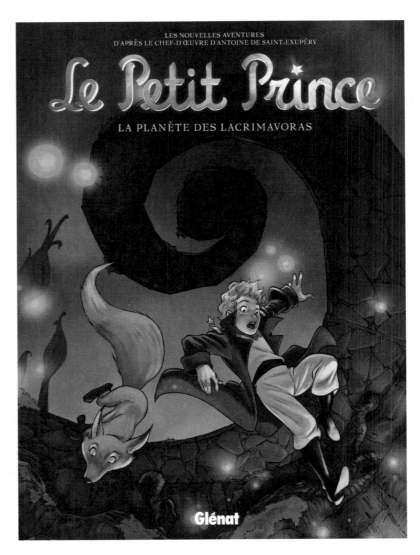

**THIS PAGE** From *The Planet of the Tear-Eaters* to *The Planet of the Grand Buffoon*, the little prince often finds himself in less than comfortable situations.

### THE PLANET OF THE CUBLIX

Lux the blacksmith is creating smog while trying to protect himself from the Cublix, whom he has mistaken for thieves. The robot-like Cublix are afraid to leave their homes, so they can't recharge their batteries. Can the little prince and the fox reconcile both parties before everything runs out of power?

### THE PLANET OF COPPELIUS

On this planet, the sun is so dazzling that some of its inhabitants lose their colors and start looking alike. Can the Little Prince convince the leader Coppelius to restore the planet's balance of shadow and sunlight?

### THE PLANET OF OKIDIANS

The asteroid Siffreo threatens to destroy the planet of the Okidians! Only the king, Okodo, can push it back into the sky with his magical powers, but he has mysteriously disappeared! Will they find Okodo before it's too late?

### THE PLANET OF ASHKABAAR

On Ashkabaar, a wall of ice separates the Crystallites from the Spherolites. Could the love that binds Shaaz and Zaac tear down the wall? The little prince and the fox will do their best to make sure it does...

### THE PLANET OF BAMALIAS

The little prince has lost his memory! The fox recounts their previous adventures so that he can continue to stop the planets from cooling down but, when the little prince comes across the snake, will the serpent mislead him?

### THE PLANET OF THE SNAKE

This time, the snake menaces the little prince's Asteroid B 612 and kidnaps the rose! Flanked by the friends he made when he helped them during his travels, the little prince will do all he can to save her. Could this be the last stand?

**LEFT** The snake who faces the little prince in a final battle does much resemble the one in Saint-Exupéry's original story.

# Comic Book Tributes

In 2006, the French monthly periodical *Lire* released several special issues to mark the 60th anniversary of the French edition of *The Little Prince*. It invited a number of prestigious comic book authors to draw their own personal interpretation of Saint-Exupéry's character. Not all famous authors had this opportunity but are included below nonetheless.

## FLORENCE CESTAC

Florence Cestac was born in 1949 and, in 1975, co-founded the comics publisher Futuropolis. Winner of the 2000 Grand Prix de la ville d'Angoulême, she writes comic books for young people (*Les Déblok*), as well as for adults, such as *Le Démon de midi* (*The Demon Stirs*) and *Un amour exemplaire* (*An Exemplary Love*).

## HUMBERTO RAMOS

Born in 1970, the Mexican illustrator is an expert on comics and has worked on superheroes such as *Spider-Man*, *Flash*, *The X-Men*, *Superman*, and *Wolverine*... yet still found time to pay homage to *The Little Prince*. Then again, in his own way, the little prince is also a kind of superhero, right?

---

**TOP** A little prince drawn by comic book illustrator Humberto Ramos.

**RIGHT** Despite the presence of his rose, Florence Cestac's little prince looks brooding and bored on his planet.

## GIPI

Born in 1963, Gian Alfonso Pacinotti, aka Gipi, won the prize for best comic book album at the Angoulême International Comics Festival in 2006 with his work *Notes For a War Story*.

## ANDRÉ JUILLARD

Born in 1948, André Juillard illustrated *Les 7 Vies de l'Épervier* (*The Seven Lives of the Sparrowhawk*), a comic series based on Patrick Cothias' text, and was one of those who revived Edgar P. Jacobs' *Blake and Mortimer*. With the fine quality of his drawings, the subtlety of his colors, and the elegant visual of his universe, Juillard's little prince is not too dissimilar to Saint-Exupéry's own.

**ABOVE** Gipi imagines the moments leading up to the aviator and the little prince meeting.

**RIGHT** André Juillard's elegant drawings are a faithful take on Saint-Exupéry's original little prince.

*Tu as du bon venin ? Tu es sûr de ne pas me faire souffrir longtemps ?*

## JUL

In *À bout de soufre*, cartoonist Jul puts a mischievous spin on some icons of popular culture, and features Saint-Exupéry's little prince in a four-page story titled *Le Grand Prince* (*The Big Prince*). Jul also illustrated *La Planète des sages* (*The Planet of Wise Men*) and its sequel, from which this excerpt is taken.

## JOANN SFAR

Born in 1971, Joann Sfar is one of the most important artists of the new wave of comic book artists which appeared in the 1990s. Beside producing over one hundred albums, including the best-selling *The Rabbi's Cat*, he is also a movie director and novelist. In 2008, he created a comic book version of *The Little Prince*, having felt a close bond with *The Little Prince* since his childhood.

*"EVERYONE HAS HIS OWN STORY WITH THIS GREAT BOOK."*
*—JOANN SFAR*

## MARTIN VEYRON

Born in 1950, Martin Veyron, who created the character of Bernard Lermite, put his sharp wit to use in making keen observations on his peers and the society of his time.

---

**ABOVE** Jul's highly ironic take on *The Little Prince*.

**BELOW** People are unlikely to mistake Joann Sfar's drawing for a hat.

**OPPOSITE PAGE** Martin Veyron reimagined and rewrote the origins of *The Little Prince*.

# The Pilot and the Little Prince

*"WHEN I WAS ASKED IF I WANTED TO RETURN TO MY COUNTRY OR STAY IN THE US, I REREAD THE LITTLE PRINCE AND I REALIZED THAT, WITH THE PILOT WHO SURVIVES IN THE DESERT, IT WAS A BOOK ABOUT COURAGE. THAT GAVE ME SO MUCH HOPE."*

Peter Sís is a poet. But he is no ordinary poet: he does not just stick to words. His work mixes words with illustration, bringing universes alive and transporting the reader on a journey, just as in Antoine Saint-Exupéry's books. His album, *The Pilot and the Little Prince*, is a magical story. On the face of it, Peter Sís is not inventing anything; he is simply telling the story of Saint-Exupéry's life. But also like *The Little Prince*, appearances can be deceiving and we should learn to see beyond them. Or rather, within them. We should let ourselves be drawn into his drawings, for his images are made up of thousands of little features, like waves in the sea or footprints in the desert.

*The Pilot and the Little Prince* stretches out across double page spreads crammed full of details and doodles which illustrate the stages of Saint-Exupérys life. Among these, big muted drawings are interposed, offering the reader a chance to rest his eyes. The text is an experience: you must turn either your head or the book to be able to read the text. The words follow the meanderings and curves of the drawings, playing leap-frog over the mountains as Saint-Exupéry used to do while flying. The text undulates over the ocean as it recounts the author's return to France in 1943 aboard the *SS Stirling Castle*. Later, when he takes off toward Spain, the hilly landscape resembles friendly debonair giants.

But where is the little prince in all that? He rides peacefully in the passenger seat of his creator's plane as it soars across the front cover, then we notice him on the final double spread, the "little boy with golden hair" who hangs onto Saint-Exupéry's plane and cycles a bicycle through the air... not unlike fellow space castaway *E.T. the Extra-terrestrial*, who left his planet to visit Earth. The wheels of his bicycle dictate the movement of the propellers. "Maybe Antoine found his own glittering planet next to the stars..." writes Sís. There is something of the little prince in the illustrator-writer. Like him, he once left his native country: in 1982, the Czechoslovakian government sent him to the US to create a movie for the 1984 Olympics. Unlike Saint-Exupéry's protagonist, however, he never returned home; he was summoned back by his country's authorities but decided to stay and live in the US.

"HE LOOKED BACK ON HIS CHILDHOOD, THE PLACES HE HAD SEEN, THE THINGS HE HAD DONE, AND THE PEOPLE HE HAD MET. HE BOUGHT A SMALL BOX OF WATERCOLORS AND BEGAN WORKING ON AN ILLUSTRATED BOOK THAT TOLD THE STORY OF A LITTLE BOY WITH GOLDEN HAIR"
—EXCERPT FROM *THE PILOT AND THE LITTLE PRINCE*

**OPPOSITE** What if the little prince had gone off with his aviator friend in his plane instead of returning to his planet?

# Le Pilote et le Petit Prince

## LA VIE
### D'ANTOINE DE SAINT-EXUPÉRY

## Peter Sís

GRASSET JEUNESSE

9- Inspired By
The Little Prince

# Merchandise

The Saint-Exupéry Estate agreed to numerous licensing agreements with brands wishing to use the image of the little prince to boost the notoriety of their products. The universal values embodied by the tale and its protagonist encapsulate the concerns of lots of companies. There are currently over 150 license holders worldwide and around 10,000 products, including Anima cuddly toys, upmarket stationery shop Le Thé des écrivains, Pixi and Leblo-Delienne figurines, Delacre biscuits, Skylantern flying paper lanterns, Kiub graphic products, Monnaie de Paris jewelry and embossed coins, Virginie tins, Bloom temporary tattoos, Moleskine notebooks, Sofitel hotels, IWC watches, Aubry Cadoret porcelain, Trousselier children's' bedroom decoration, Plastoy toys, Buzzebizz smartphone accessories... Not to mention authentic baobabs imported from Senegal or the little prince's rose, cultivated by Delbard and sold with proceeds going to the non-profit association Petits Princes.

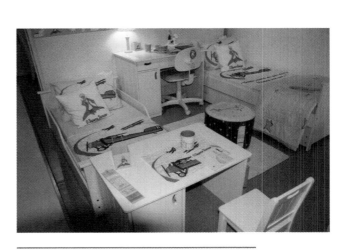

**PRECEDING PAGES** Little prince and fox, Collectoys.

**TOP** *Little Prince* lockets and bracelets, Monnaie de Paris.

**CENTER** *Little Prince* lampshade, Trousselier.

**ABOVE** *Little Prince*-themed bedroom.

**LEFT** *Little Prince* calendars, Fleurus.

**TOP** Line of *Little Prince* notebooks, Fleurus.

**ABOVE RIGHT** Ball-point "sheep" pen, Zéphyr.

**BELOW** Pen, Petit Jour – Paris.

**BELOW, CENTER** Pair of little prince figurines, Pixi.

**RIGHT** Selection of figurines, Pixi.

**BOTTOM LEFT** Little prince figurine, Art Toy.

**ABOVE** *Little Prince* toys, Tap Ball 2000.

**TOP RIGHT** Christmas biscuit boxes, Delacre, 2015.

**RIGHT** Jack-in-the-box and lamp, Trousselier.

These products, along with their manufacturing and distribution conditions, must adhere to the values encapsulated by Antoine de Saint-Exupéry's work. As such, articles under Mexican and Brazilian licenses are made in Mexico and Brazil, in accordance with principals of sustainable development. Foreign manufacturing must respect the Convention on the Rights of the Child, adopted by the United Nations General Assembly in 1989.

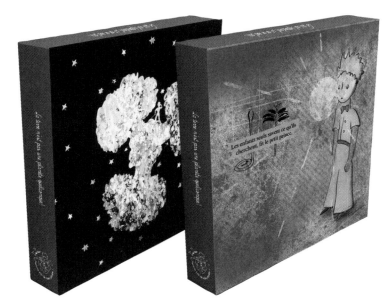

**ABOVE** Limited-edition sculpture, Neamedia.

**TOP RIGHT** *Little Prince* canvases, Paristic studio.

**BELOW** *Little Prince* coin bank, Plastoy.

**BOTTOM RIGHT** Costumes for children and adults, Chaks.

161

NOUS ECRIVONS DES CHOSES ETERNELLES

**TOP** Wall stickers, Paristic/Déco minus.

**RIGHT** *Little Prince*-themed baobabs, Végétaux d'ailleurs (Senegal).

**BELOW** *The Little Prince* postcards, Huginn&Muninn.

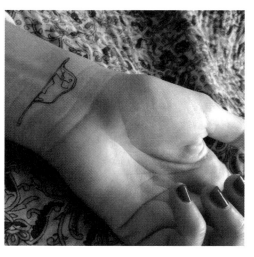

**TOP** Gift set of cild dishes in Saint-Exupéry watercolor shades. Petit Jour – Paris.

**BOTTOM LEFT** Stuffed toys, Sekiguchi.

**ABOVE** Temporary tattoo. Bloom.

# Learning with The Little Prince

## LEARN FRENCH WITH *THE LITTLE PRINCE*

The little prince knows no borders. Not only has his tale been translated and published in many countries, it has also played its part in uniting people otherwise separated by language barriers. Several bilingual editions set out to help readers learn French. They are aimed at Korean, Romanian, and Chinese readers and add explanations and vocabulary notes around Saint-Exupéry's tale.

## "PLEASE—DRAW ME A SHEEP..."

Learning to say, "Please—draw me a sheep" in English is easy... if you can read the Romanian! Complete with songs, poems, conversations, and a dictionary—all accompanied by Natalia Conran's illustrations—Despina Calavrezo's collection *English with The Little Prince* is aimed at helping Romanian children familiarize themselves with the language of Shakespeare.

**ABOVE** The game by Ludonaute inspired by the Mark Osborne animated film.

**BOTTOM LEFT** This method of learning English is aimed at Romanian readers and based on Saint-Exupéry's tale.

## PLAY WITH THE LITTLE PRINCE

From games publisher Ludonaute comes this interactive board game inspired by *The Little Prince* universe. The game is suitable for two to five players, aged eight years and up (grown-ups can play, too!).

The objective is simple: use tiles to build the prettiest of planets and then foxes, sheep, roses... or an elephant.

Following the release of Mark Osborne's animated feature, Ludonaute created another game, *The Little Prince –Rising to the Stars*. Designed for two and six players (aged six and up), each player boards an airplane and follows the lead of the little girl from the movie: the goal is to reach the little prince's planet and find him.

### *I LEARN TO READ WITH THE LITTLE PRINCE* (FLEURUS)

Kindergarten and elementary school aged children are in luck! *The Little Prince* is ready and waiting to be discovered in this version of Saint-Exupéry's text which has been adapted especially for young children. Its vocabulary and comprehension notes were written by an elementary school teacher and are designed to help children progress easily through reading the story and learning to write... and, with pages of games, to have fun at the same time! This book will no doubt have you longing for your elementary school days...

---

**TOP LEFT** An interactive game that has readers dreaming up planets like Saint-Exupéry.

**RIGHT** It is never too early to discover *The Little Prince*, especially if it helps young children to read.

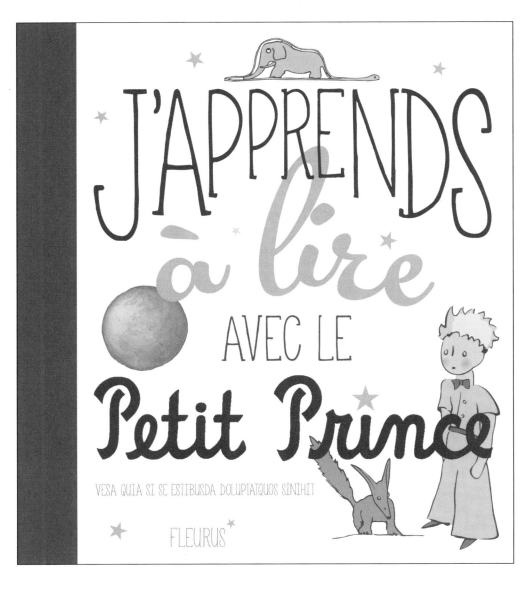

### I COUNT SHEEP WITH THE LITTLE PRINCE (FLEURUS)

One sheep, two sheep, three sheep... Anyone trying to send a baby to sleep need only reach for this book. There is no better way to send them drifting into wonderful dreams with the little prince and the fox.

### I CAN COUNT WITH THE LITTLE PRINCE (GALLIMARD)

If you want to count sheep, you have to start by learning numbers...

**ABOVE** Although the little prince in Saint-Exupéry's tale has just one sheep, there are plenty more out there to help send babies to sleep.

**RIGHT** An adapted vocabulary allows even young children to explore the universe of *The Little Prince*.

**LEFT** With this book, you do not need to be a businessman to learn how to count!

### THE LITTLE PRINCE FOR BABIES (FLEURUS)

Children of all ages can get to know Antoine de Saint-Exupéry's tale thanks to this large-print version with vocabulary chosen especially for small children.

## I DISCOVER... WITH THE LITTLE PRINCE (FLEURUS)
*I Discover Colors, I Discover Opposites, I Discover Manners, I Discover Animals...*

A collection accompanying little ones as they learn life skills.

## THE LITTLE PRINCE PICTURE BOOK (FLEURUS)
Stars, sheep, rose, sun... Learn around 20 new words with the little prince.

**ABOVE** Discover colors with the little prince.

**RIGHT** A picture book to help learn words and how to say, "Please—draw me a sheep."

# Jean-Charles de Castelbajac, Prince of Fashion

One look at Pharrell Williams' hat may leave us asking wondering, and rightly so, what if, instead of being a hat, it was a picture of a boa constrictor digesting an elephant?

A glance, however, at some of Jean-Charles de Castelbajac's creations leaves no room for doubt—they are very clearly an homage to Antoine de Saint-Exupéry.

His Spring 2011 collection was devoted to the themes of aviation and travel, and featured models strutting their stuff in shirts bearing the little prince's portrait. Others were dressed in kaftans with book cover images from *Night Flight* and *Wind, Sand and Stars* from Éditions Gallimard's famous "white collection".

*"I WAS 17 WHEN I STARTED OUT IN THE FASHION INDUSTRY AND SO I WAS KNOWN AS THE LITTLE PRINCE. ALL MY LIFE, I'VE BEEN CONFRONTED BY HIS IMAGE."*   —JEAN-CHARLES DE CASTELBAJAC

References to the world of childhood, art, and important figures in popular imagery have always featured in the work of "JC/DC" who takes interest in all things popular. However, that was not his sole motivation for using the universe of Saint-Exupéry in his collection. The couturier felt a close bond with *The Little Prince*. When he was 14, he discovered a copy of the book dedicated by the author to his father. Having been sent to boarding school between the ages of five and 17 and deprived of his childhood and teenage years, the young de Castelbajac immediately felt a connection between the protagonist's solitude and his own—a feeling that made up his daily life at boarding school and bound him to Saint-Exupéry's main character. "*The Little Prince* was my first work, my cornerstone," he would explain in 2011 during an interview with the website thelittleprince.com.

It was not just the words of "Saint-Ex's" story that struck de Castelbajac, but the graphic dimension. "One very touching illustration of Saint-Exupéry's made me think of a quote from Cervantes, 'Always keep a hold of the child you once were,'" continued the designer. "Whether he draws well or not is irrelevant. We are not here to draw well, or to do pretty things; we are here to create things that are disturbing." Jean-Charles de Castelbajac has come across several "little princes" in his life, like New York artists Jean-Michel Basquiat and Keith Haring. He who had been behind the costumes for Richard Cocciante's show dreamed of making a Broadway-style musical. But his would be one of contemporary inspiration, "made of electro-rock energy" and that would send a message of hope to young generations.

*"I HAVE A REAL SOFT SPOT FOR [THE LITTLE PRINCE]. HIS ADVENTURE IS LIKE A MELANCHOLY BIBLE, A ROAD MOVIE OF SOLITUDE."*
*—JEAN-CHARLES*
*DE CASTELBAJAC*

Proceeds from the sale of his collection went to The Antoine de Saint-Exupéry Youth Foundation. According to de Castelbajac, the Foundation is a good idea which, he believes, "Antoine would agree with. If there is a cause for fighting for, it's that of young people", one of Jean-Charles de Castelbajac's principal concerns. "It's good that the Saint-Exupéry Foundation is devoted to this idea which is so strong and typical of Saint-Exupéry: we are just passing through; we borrow the earth from our children."

**OPPOSITE AND PRECEDING PAGES** Available in short sleeve or long sleeve, Jean-Charles de Castelbajac decorative shirts are emblazoned with Saint-Exupéry's young hero.

**ABOVE** Who says literature and fashion don't mix? These kaftans bearing the cover images of *Wind, Sand and Stars* and *Night Flight* blend the two.

# The Little Prince in Advertising

Please—draw me an advertisement...
Images of Antoine de Saint-Exupéry's
little hero have appeared in promotional
materials, from S.T. Dupont cigarette
lighters to French electricity provider EDF.
In addition, Réunica, a non-profit social
security group, notably featured the little
prince sweeping his volcano as part of
their campaign to encourage alternative
medicines to help those who quit
smoking. Veolia, a French multinational
whose activities include water and energy
management and waste treatment,
featured him in an attempt to highlight
the vital importance of preserving the
environment for the sake of our planet's
future, for which we are all responsible.

THIS PAGE Some of the images used in Toshiba's Japanese advertising campaign.

In Japan, a TV commercial for low-energy light bulbs as a means of saving electricity, portrayed the little prince in a cartoon which evoked the drawing style of Saint-Exupéry. This partnership with the Japanese company Toshiba affirmed the little prince's image as a proponent of sustainable development. The little prince is not incompatible with advertising, as long as it is line with his ideals.

**TOP LEFT** One of the Réunica advertisements in the style of *The Little Prince*.

**BOTTOM LEFT** The little prince sleeps peacefully in this advertisement for Air France.

**ABOVE** By taking care of his planet, the little prince set an example and was a precursor of the move towards sustainable development.

eFrance

프랑스

랑스문화딸

10- The Little Prince
Around the World

# The Little Prince Theme Park

*DISCOVERED 70 YEARS AGO BY A TURKISH ASTRONOMER, ASTEROID B 612 LANDED IN ALSACE IN SUMMER 2014.*

A labyrinth, two tethered hot-air balloons, an aerobar, and a family of foxes... Plus three cinemas, a trampoline field, flocks of sheep, flying chairs... This list, as if from Jacques Prevert's *Inventaire*, gives some idea of the varied program which awaits visitors to the Parc du Petit Prince (Little Prince Park) in Ungerheim, France, in the Alsace region between the cities of Colmar and Mulhouse. As the world's first aerial theme park, it promises visitors a journey at least as surprising and disorienting as Saint-Exupéry's character's interplanetary voyage!

**PREVIOUS PAGE** "When I came back from my work the next evening, I saw from some distance away my little prince sitting on top of a wall, with his feet dangling." (*The Little Prince*, Chapter 26)

**ABOVE** A hot-air balloon offers breathtaking views of the Alsatian countryside.

**LEFT** The Little Prince Park, the world's first aerial theme park, welcomes you!

**BELOW** An ideal amusement park for children and families.

Opened to the public on July 1, 2014 and underwritten by Yannick Noah, the park was designed by Aerophile SAS, a company specialized in the installation and use of tethered balloons. It was installed on the former site of Bioscope, an environmental theme park which ran from 2006 to 2012. Its circular shape brings to mind a meteorite crater, and from this we can imagine that Asteroid B 612 really could have crashed in this exact spot. Two planet-balloons and an aerobar orbiting the park, shall we say, seem to have their respective natives: a king, a lamplighter, and a drunkard.

TOP The aerobar would have delighted the drunkard from *The Little Prince*.

ABOVE The biggest biplane in the world awaits imitators of Saint-Exupéry for a journey in the skies.

LEFT An attraction which gives you wings, inspired by *Night Flight*.

The 30 or so attractions in the park evoke the Saint-Exupéry universe: from the "Drunkard's Aerobar" to "Tame Me" to "The Lamplighter's Balloon"; from "Draw me a sheep", to "*Southern Mail*", "*Citadel* (*The Wisdom of the Sands*)" and "B 612". They are arranged according to four themes: Flying, Animals, Exploring, and Gardens.

www.parcdupetitprince.com

## ANIMALS

Cross paths with real sheep and draw one of them on the circular wall; visit the fox cubs born in the park; see a caterpillar change into a butterfly; get to know the birds personally...

## FLYING

Plunge into the void; discover gravity; have a drink 155 feet in the air; climb 490 feet over the planet (or rather let the lamplighter's planet balloon do it for you); take a trip on a biplane which could have belonged to Antoine de Saint-Exupéry; ride out a storm in the middle of the night to relive the experience of an Aéropostale pilot...

**TOP LEFT** A science quiz to help the Turkish astronomer answer the (many) questions that he has on his mind.

**TOP RIGHT** Aerial view of The Little Prince Park.

**ABOVE** Standing on his planet, the little prince seems to be contemplating the theme park that bears his name.

## EXPLORING

Cross the park in a miniature train; dodge the traps on a giant hopscotch grounds to deliver mail to the other side of the Earth; help the astronomer find answers to all of his questions; watch a screening of *The Wings of Courage*, Jean-Jacques Annaud's film dedicated to Henri Guillaumet; travel under the sea on a 4D expedition...

**ABOVE** Thanks to the king's planet balloon, you can admire the sunset from 490 feet.

**BELOW LEFT** ...As long as you're not afraid of heights!

**BELOW RIGHT** "It was then that the fox appeared." (*The Little Prince*, Chapter 21)

*EACH SATELLITE SEEMS TO HAVE ITS RESPECTIVE NATIVE: A KING, A LAMPLIGHTER, AND A DRUNKARD.*

## GARDENS

Stroll through the butterfly gardens; examine Asteroid B 612 up close; discover the roses from *The Little Prince* reunited in the rose garden; lose yourself in the maze which leads to the spring of fresh water; enjoy the water from the desert well...

# And Elsewhere?

Not even in his wildest dreams could Antoine de Saint-Exupéry have imagined that his character would become so famous after his death. Today, the little prince is celebrated around the world, in many unexpected places. He is always at home on our planet! He has lent his name to innumerous educational establishments, nurseries, streets, hotels and restaurants, and that's to say nothing of the statues, sculptures, and murals which pay him tribute. This genuine citizen of the world thus proves the universal appeal of Saint-Exupéry's tale. His stay on Earth may have been brief, but the mark that he left in the hearts of mankind shows no signs of fading...

## THE PEQUENO PRÍNCIPE HOSPITAL (BRAZIL)

In Curitiba, the state capital of Paraná, the Pequeno Principe Hospital (The Little Prince Hospital) is the biggest pediatric establishment in Brazil. Inspired by the values of Saint-Exupéry, it aims to provide the same level of attention to the children entrusted to its care as the hero of the story gives his rose. The young patients benefit from a structure specially adapted to their needs. Teachers, actors, and volunteers are tasked with helping them to forget their medical conditions to make their stay and their treatment easier by helping "tame" their illness with them.

The hospital is committed to the eight Millennium Development goals adopted by the United Nations in 2000. To celebrate the 70th anniversary of *The Little Prince*, it launched the Criando Iacos (Creating Bonds) project with the production of a giant fresco and a book, and a series of drawings displayed in May 2014 at the United Nations headquarters in New York.

www.pequenoprincipe.org.br/hospital

## HAKONE MUSEUM (JAPAN)

On June 29, 1999, Antoine de Saint-Exupéry would have been 99 years old. On this date, a museum dedicated to the man and his works, particularly *The Little Prince*, opened in Japan. Located in Hakone, west of Tokyo, it was founded by Akiko Torii, a great admirer of the writer. The museum offers a complete immersion in his universe, and features identical reproductions of some of the writer's favorite places..

The entrance of the park, where visitors are welcomed by a statue of the little prince on his planet, is a replica of the gateway to the château in Saint-Maurice-de-Rémens, whose façade is reproduced in a full-scale mock-up, as is his childhood home in Lyon. Four key places from Saint-Exupéry's life are represented: his childhood bedroom at Saint-Maurice, complete with toys;

the room in Cape Juby where he wrote *Southern Mail*; his Aéropostale office in Buenos Aires where he drafted *Night Flight*; and finally the bedroom from his New York apartment on Central Park South. Also on display is a replica of the plane that he piloted for Aéropostale. Even the café, the Saint-Germain-des-Près, was modeled on his favorite Parisian establishment, the Brasserie Lipp; while a chapel located in the museum grounds resembles the one found near the Château de Saint-Maurice.

The exhibition room contains photographs tracing the life and career of Saint-Exupéry, handwritten letters, original illustrations made while *The Little Prince* was being written, and various editions of the story. The decor evokes the different stages of his travels, taking inspiration from Moroccan, Argentinian, Parisian, and American settings. You can hear the voice of the writer, recorded while advising movie director Jean Renoir on an adaptation of *Wind, Sand and Stars*.

At the end of the visit, after a detour to the Little Prince Theatre and the restaurant of the same name, visitors are invited to browse the souvenirs offered at the Five Hundred Million Little Bells Boutique, the name of which references the last chapter of the famous tale by Saint-Exupéry.

http://www.tbs.co.jp/l-prince/en/

**OPPOSITE PAGE** The little prince welcomes visitors in person to the Hakone Museum in Japan.

지리학자

"우리는 꽃 따위는 기록하지 않는단다,
꽃은 덧없는 것이기 때문이야." —어린왕자 중에서—

## PETITE FRANCE (SOUTH KOREA)

As a Korean CEO with a love for both France (which he has visited more than 50 times) and *The Little Prince*, Mr. Han combined his passions to build, from scratch, a village called... Petite (Little) France. Located near Lake Gapyeoung, about 40 miles from Seoul, the capital of South Korea, the site gives visitors the opportunity to discover different facets of French culture through its various houses. Visitors are welcomed by a statue of the little prince (*Orin Wanja*, in Korean), who is very popular in South Korea, where more than 350 editions of the story have been published. In the streets, there are murals and statues depicting the characters. There is also a three-story house devoted to a permanent exhibition of the life and works of Saint-Exupéry, who simultaneously embodies the literature, style, and spirit of France in the eyes of Mr. Han. A theatrical version of the tale is put on for children every weekend, whilst a screening room plays musicals, films, operas, or plays adapted from *The Little Prince*.

## THE TARFAYA MUSEUM (MOROCCO)

Situated in the south of Morocco between the waves of the Atlantic and the dunes of the Sahara, Cape Juby-Tarfaya was a regular stopover for pilots to refuel their Bréguet 14s as they carried mail between Toulouse and Saint-Louis, Senegal. Since 2004, this has been the site of a Saint-Exupéry museum, which retraces the saga of Aéropostale and recalls the role of "Saint-Ex" as a negotiator with Moorish tribes. A monument pays tribute to the aviator-writer. The idea for *The Little Prince* was perhaps conceived here, amongst the sand and the light of the desert, before becoming fixed in his mind 15 years later, during his stay in the United States.

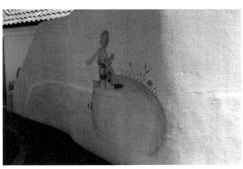

**OPPOSITE PAGE** At the risk of surprising actual geographers, Petite France is situated... in South Korea.

**TOP RIGHT** Even the little prince needs a touch up from time to time.

**ABOVE** The whole area is painted in the colors of *The Little Prince*, recalling the watercolors of Saint-Exupéry.

**LEFT** Culture shock is guaranteed for Korean visitors who are unfamiliar with France.

## YORII REST STOP (JAPAN)

Since June 29, 2010, Japanese motorists who take the highway past Yorii in the prefecture of Saitama can take advantage of a 66,000 sq. ft rest stop dedicated to *The Little Prince* universe. Conceived by Akiko Torii, the founder of the Hakone museum, this space offers a restaurant named the The Little Prince, a Saint-Exupéry cafe, a flower shop called Ephémère, as well as a "capricious shop". Before getting back on the road, stroll through the garden: between a burrow (for the fox), a vineyard for the "impatient drunkard", street lamps, and a splendid yellow rose (marked Saint-Exupéry), it provides the opportunity for a soothing walk in the story's universe.

**TOP** Having explored several planets, the little prince is at home at the Yorii rest stop in Japan.

**ABOVE** The little prince surrounded by roses, as in the story of Saint-Exupéry.

**LEFT** Step inside The Little Prince restaurant…

## THE LITTLE PRINCE AT THE GREVIN MUSEUM (FRANCE, CANADA)

The little prince really does exist! Not only can you see the evidence, you can get up close and even touch him… or, at least the statue made of resin and laminated polyester on display at the Grevin Museum in Paris since December 14, 2011. Flanked by the fox and his rose, he was modeled by the sculptor and visual artist Stéphane Barret, based on the character from the animated series broadcast on France 3. The result is surprising: visitors truly feel as if they are standing face to face with the hero of the saga, with his blond locks, his baggy trousers, and the constellations on his coat, made of shiny little "jewels" sewn on one-by-one.

All that he is missing is speech and the ability to come to life… "He is positively alive, we see this character that we have known forever," declared Olivier d'Agay, director of the Saint-Exupéry Estate, at the statue's unveiling. "There he is, a little boy in the flesh… You want to take him in your arms!" So now you can take a selfie with the little prince! The aviator of the story didn't have the chance: he had to be content with drawing him from memory. In 2013, another likeness of the little prince was presented to the Grevin Museum in Montreal, Canada.

www.grevin.com

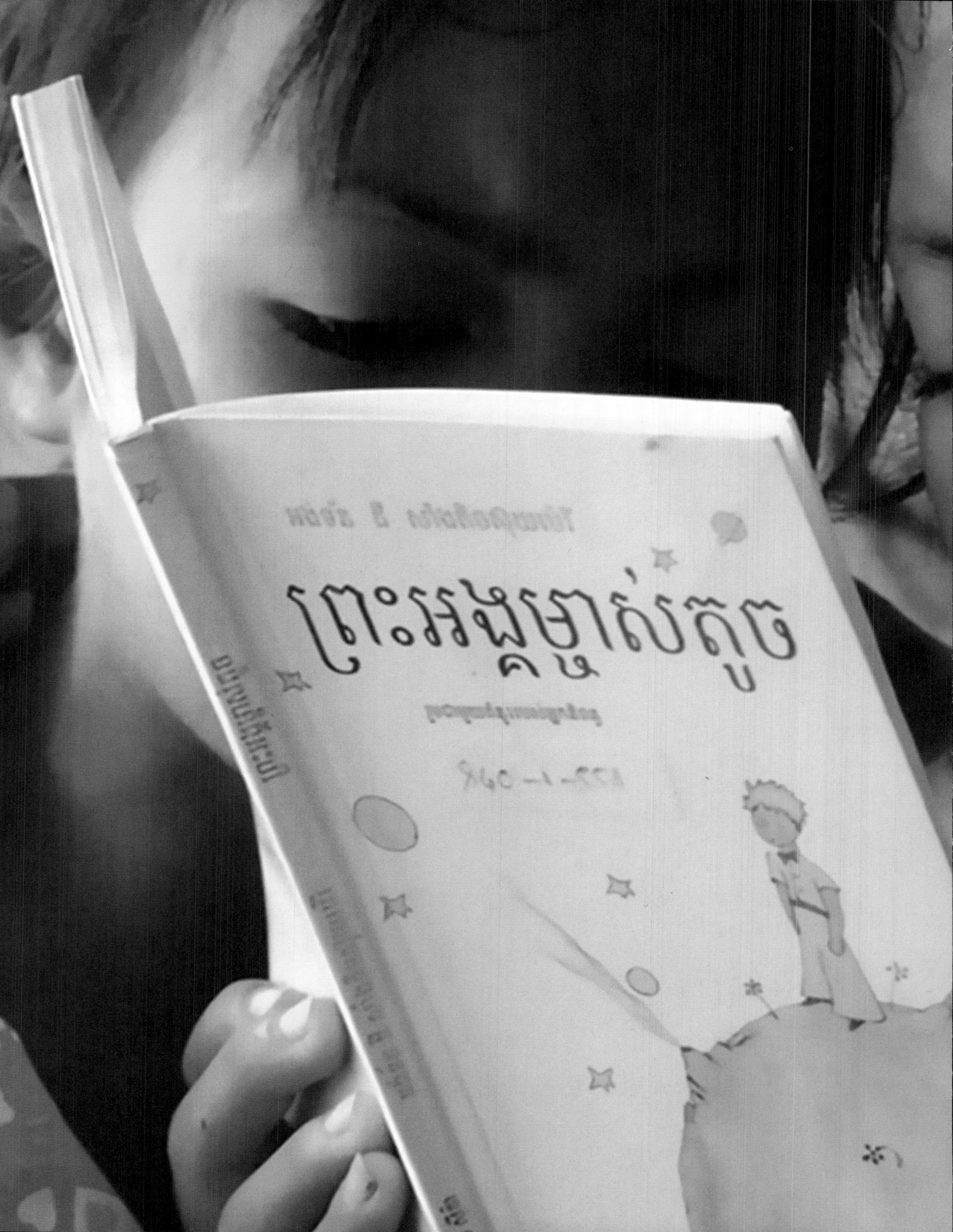
ព្រះអង្គម្ចាស់តូច

11- The Little
Prince and Us

# Everyone Loves The Little Prince !

The magic of drawing knows no bounds. And if *The Little Prince* is universal, the same may also be said of its admirers, who come from all over the world.

There is no need to implore them, "Please—draw me a little prince": they do it spontaneously, thus testifying to the enduring fascination and attachment aroused by Saint-Exupéry's character.

**PREVIOUS SPREAD** The SIPAR association fights illiteracy in Cambodia: a little girl discovers *The Little Prince*.

**FROM LEFT TO RIGHT, TOP TO BOTTOM**
*Flower with Millions of Stars* by Platynews.
*The Little Prince* by Megatruh.
*The Little Prince* by Ryouworld.
*The Little Prince* by Poevil.

*"FOR YOU WHO ALSO LOVE THE LITTLE PRINCE, AND FOR ME, NOTHING IN THE UNIVERSE CAN BE THE SAME IF SOMEWHERE, WE DO NOT KNOW WHERE, A SHEEP THAT WE NEVER SAW HAS— YES OR NO?—EATEN A ROSE…"*

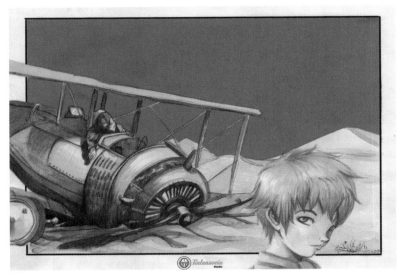

**FROM LEFT TO RIGHT, TOP TO BOTTOM**
*The Little Prince* by Israel Maia.
*Little Prince* by Caio Souza "Yo".
*The Little Prince* by HyeinGo.
*Plane Crash The Little Prince*, by Bartok.
*Untitled* by Niko Geyer.

**COUNTERCLOCKWISE, FROM TOP RIGHT**
*The Little Prince* by Breno de Borba.
*My little prince* by Wibblequibble.
*The Little Prince* by Neemh.

Little prince fan art from the world over combines different graphic influences and sources of inspiration in drawings, watercolors, or collages; and also through photos, clay figures, 3D objects, clothing, cosplay, or even... cakes. These readers and fans display their work on *The Little Prince* Facebook page, before being published every Friday on lepetitprince.com as part of Fan Art Friday. So, grab your pencils...and let your imagination guide you.

**TOP** *Untitled* by MasterTeacher.
**RIGHT** *Little Prince* by Юлия Броновицкая.

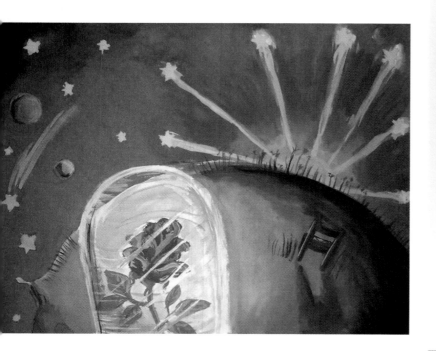

**CLOCKWISE, FROM TOP LEFT**

*Little Prince Loves Sunsets* by Oruba.
*The Little Prince* by Vifon.
*Untitled* by Gally.

*"PLEASE COMFORT ME.*
*SEND ME WORD THAT HE*
*HAS COME BACK…"*

**TOP TO BOTTOM**
*The Little Prince With Me* by Charles Floria.
*The Prince and the Fox* by Pokita.
*The Little Prince, The Fox* by Pilar Hernández.

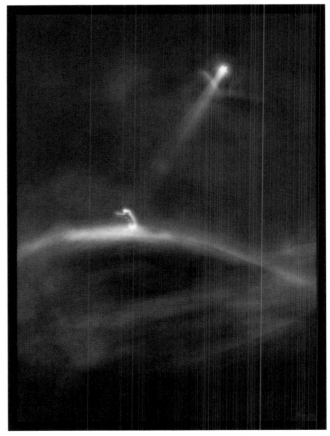

**COUNTERCLOCKWISE, FROM TOP RIGHT**

*Untitled* by famoalmehairi.
*The Little Prince* by Yasemin Ezberci.
*The Little Prince* by Muesliriegel.

**FROM LEFT TO RIGHT, TOP TO BOTTOM**
*Untitled* by Elle duPomme.
*The Little Prince* by Pablo Olivero.
*Untitled* by Élodie Stervinou.
*The Little Prince* by Marina Simunovic.

# Collectors

The Little Prince collectors form a real community, with members spread all over the world. Thanks to the internet, they can expand their collections, swap items, and discuss their mutual passion. And, as some of them are also big travellers, they also go to visit each other and develop friendships, following the example of the little prince and Saint-Exupéry.

But their aim isn't necessarily to amass the greatest number of volumes like the businessman hoarding his stars. Instead, they follow the lesson of the fox, seeking to forge bonds between all those who love Saint-Exupéry's work. Hence, Turkish collector Yildiroay Lise dreams of opening a museum dedicated to *Küçük Prens* (*The Little Prince*) in Ankara. In the meantime, he celebrated the 71st anniversary of the character by helping to organize an exhibition in Istanbul, which was notable for displaying the first Turkish translation of Saint-Exupéry's text. In 2009, Italian Antonio Massimo Fragomeni explained on the official *Little Prince* website that his hundreds of copies, in more than a hundred languages, constitutes "a collection of bonds" and that, in essence, a network of friends has developed all around the world thanks to the tale. Patrick Tourreau, in France, thinks that his collection of hundreds of volumes, which take up meters and meters of shelving in his personal library, represents all of humankind, which could be assembled "on a small Pacific islet," as Saint-Exupéry mused in Chapter 17 of *The Little Prince.*

*"I AM MORE THAN A COLLECTOR. MY AIM IS TO SPREAD THE MESSAGE OF THE LITTLE PRINCE TO OTHER POPULATIONS, OTHER PEOPLE. THAT'S WHY I DO NEW TRANSLATIONS EVERY YEAR"*
*—JEAN-MARC PROBST.*

**ABOVE** The personal libraries of these collectors (such as that of Jean-Marc Probst, shown) sometimes contain thousands of first editions.

Jaume Arboné, from the Catalonia region of Spain, also has several hundred first editions in dozens of different languages. To him, little-spoken language from all around the world must be protected; they represent humanity's heritage. Arboné helps to preserve them by translating and publishing The Little Prince in

threatened languages such as Aranese, an Occitan dialect spoken by 2,000 people in the Aran Valley in Catalonia. He also provides financial backing for new translations and helps foreign publishers to build partnerships with Gallimard, who hold the international rights to Saint-Exupéry's famous story.

Collectors do not only look for official editions: Michael Pättel from Germany, whose "treasure trove" consists of more than 2,000 books, is also interested in "pirate" versions. These offer new illustrations and translations which serve to enrich the work. It is not the feeling of accumulation or an obsession

to beat records that motivates him; it's more his curiosity about the variety of drawings and words that the original *Little Prince* has inspired.

But the uncontested record holder remains Swiss Jean-Marc Probst: his collection, started in 1980, brings together more than 3,400 different editions in 270 languages and dialects! And that's not to mention exhibition programs, musical scores, posters, magazines, scripts, and all sorts of audiovisual materials. His website (www.petit-prince-collection.com) is a mine of information and he even created a foundation in 2013. The aim of the website is twofold: to allow public access to his items, and to increase the sphere of influence of Saint-Exupéry's works through new translations and publications. And so, in 2008, Jean-Marc Probst translated *The Little Prince* into Ticinese (a dialect found in

Italian-speaking areas of Switzerland) and then, two years later, into Somali (spoken in the horn of Africa). This list of enthusiasts is by no means exhaustive. You only have to scroll through the official Facebook group for friends of *The Little Prince*, or take a look at the list of International Friends of The Little Prince compiled by Patrick Tourreau (www.patoche.org/lepetitprince) to see. And anyone may come and join the ranks, regardless of the size of their collection, as long as they share the same passion. After all, what is essential is invisible to the eye.

**TOP** The collection of Jean-Marc Probst, as impressive as the businessman's collection of stars! Since 1980, he has assembled more than 3,400 different editions of *The Little Prince*.

**ABOVE** A library, or a representation of humankind that could be gathered all together "on a small Pacific islet"?

# The Little Prince and Society

## THE LITTLE PRINCE AND CHILDREN'S RIGHTS

Tolerance, respect for other cultures, children's rights... All these themes are at the heart of Antoine de Saint-Exupéry's tale. From February 3 to March 20, 2014, to mark Francophone Month and Black History Month, *The Little Prince* was chosen to be the emblematic figure of a writing competition, based on the themes of human and children's rights, for pupils at the French Heritage Language Program in New York. The character chosen for the poster was none other than the black little prince found on the cover of *Masadennin*, the translation of Saint-Exupéry's tale into Bambara, the main language spoken in Mali. What makes him so original? The prince's blond locks remain but he is dressed in a white costume and has black skin.

---

**TOP LEFT** This black little prince was initially found on the cover of *Masadennin*, the Bambara translation of the tale.

**TOP RIGHT** A rendering of the Sentinel Space Telescope.

## THE B 612 FOUNDATION

The B 612 Foundation is an American foundation established in 2002 with two main purposes: to map the trajectories of asteroids that risk colliding with the earth and to find the technological means to divert their path to avoid such collisions. The foundation announced its plans to launch the Sentinel Space Telescope, designed to locate asteroids that pose a potential threat, in 2017 or 2018. While some may only measure a foot or so in diameter, others can be several hundred miles long. The most dangerous among them measure more than 500 feet long, and are classed as near-Earth objects if they pass within... 28 million miles of the Earth.

In 2002, French astronaut Philippe Perrin traveled to the International Space Station, taking with him just one book: *The Little Prince*. Three asteroids commemorate "Saint-Ex" and his work, named rather straightforwardly by scientists as "Saint-Exupéry", "Little Prince", and "Bésixdouze". This list of tributes grew in 1995 when the International Astronomical Union named another asteroid "4049 (Noragal)" in homage to Nora Gal (full name Eleonora Yaklovena Galperina), who created the first Russian translation of *The Little Prince*.

Never fear, the "real" Asteroid B 612 imagined by "Saint-Ex" is far too small to ever pose a threat to humanity. If it were, however, to come closer to our planet one day, perhaps we might finally get a close look at the little prince...

## CURRENCY EVENTS

In France, a 50-Franc bank note featuring the little prince, the illustration of the elephant swallowed by the boa constrictor, and a portrait of their creator was released in homage to Antoine de Saint-Exupéry. Designed in 1992 by the French-Swiss painter and graphic artist Roger Pfund, the note remained in circulation from 1993 to 2001. Some of the notes printed in 1992 and 1993 bear a spelling mistake, with an acute accent on the first "E" of "Exupéry". The error was corrected in 1997 when a new bank note was produced.

Le Petit Prince

Une action de diplomatie culturelle

A cultural diplomacy initiative

**LEFT** The cover of the brochure presenting the cultural diplomacy initiative for which the little prince served as an emblem.

**BELOW** The 50-Franc bank note bearing Saint-Exupéry's portrait, designed in 1992.

## THE LITTLE PRINCE, A UNIVERSAL SYMBOL

March 2014 was Francophonie Month. In celebration of the occasion, a cultural diplomacy initiative selected the little prince as its emblem. The Permanent Representation of the International Organization of La Francophonie (IOF) to the United Nations in New York; the Outreach Division, Department of Public Information at the United Nations; the Quebec Government Office in New York; and the Estate of Antoine de Saint-Exupéry have all used Saint-Exupéry's character as a means of defending the universal values which drive the UN and IOF to act.

The little prince bears a humanist message transcending national, cultural, and religious differences; speaks a simple, universal language, and is globally renowned thanks to multiple translations. Saint-Exupéry's protagonist is the ideal ambassador for uniting Earth's inhabitants, strengthening the ties that bind humans to nature, promoting diversity, and bringing a fresh perspective to the way we regard our planet.

# Exhibitions

## THE MORGAN LIBRARY (NEW YORK)

From January through April, 2014, the Morgan Library & Museum, home to the original manuscript of *The Little Prince*, ran an exhibition entitled *The Little Prince: A New York Story*. Featuring extracts from Antoine de Saint-Exupéry's manuscript, unseen writings, photographs, illustrations, watercolors, letters, and artifacts—such as his chain bracelet, discovered by a fisherman in 1998—the exhibition retraced the origins of *The Little Prince*.

The story of *The Little Prince* is closely linked to New York City. It was there that the tale was written and first published, both in its original French and its English translation. The exhibition included readings of the story, activities for children, as well as a screening of Will Vinton's short film adaptation.

www.themorgan.org

**ABOVE** Photographs of Antoine de Saint-Exupéry as a pilot, taken during his final missions, on show in New York.

**LEFT** The poster for The Morgan Library & Museum's exhibition in New York.

*SAINT-EXUPÉRY, DECKED OUT IN HIS MILITARY UNIFORM, TURNED UP AT HIS FRIEND SILVIA HAMILTON'S DOOR. "I WANT TO GIVE YOU HAVE SOMETHING SPLENDID, BUT THIS IS ALL I HAVE," HE ANNOUNCED, TOSSING A RUMPLED PAPER BAG ON HER ENTRY HALL TABLE. INSIDE WERE THE ORIGINAL MANUSCRIPT AND DRAWINGS FOR* THE LITTLE PRINCE, *WHICH THE MORGAN LIBRARY & MUSEUM ACQUIRED IN 1968.*

## ARLUDIK (PARIS)

To mark the release of Mark Osborne's full-length animated feature film *The Little Prince*, the Arludik gallery in Paris ran an exhibition from June 19 to September19, 2015 entitled *The Art of The Little Prince*. On show were drawings from the movie's development stages, and around 100 works signed by Peter de Sève and Alexander Juhasz were available for purchase. Peter de Sève was the head of character design and Alexander Juhasz produced magnificent watercolor and pencil drawings used in the production of the stop-motion animated scenes.

www.arludik.com

**ABOVE** Four studies of the little prince's expressions and attitudes by Alexander Juhasz.

**RIGHT** We read in the fox's expression the close bond shared by he and the little prince in this sketch by Peter de Sève, the artist who designed he characters in Mark Osborne's movie.

# Non-Profit Organizations

## PETITS PRINCES

Whether it's swimming with dolphins, meeting a sports star in person, shaking the hand of a favorite celebrity, cooking up a storm with a top chef, cuddling a koala, or climbing aboard an airplane... every child has a dream! Since 1987, the charitable association Petits Princes has been working to make dreams come true for children suffering from cancer, leukemia, or genetic diseases. Teaming up with the child's family and partnering with medical teams, the charity is there for every step of the child's treatment. Their volunteers help children find new strength to battle their illness. Between 1988 and 2014, 5,300 wishes came true for 2,500 children. Petits Princes is the initiative of Dominique Bayle, a physical education teacher and ski instructor, who always believed in the power of her project and in the importance of childhood dreams.

www.petitsprinces.com

## DESSINE-MOI UN MOUTON

Since 1990, this association has been working with children, teenagers, and young adults afflicted by AIDS or other contagious diseases. In this place of welcome, they are supported throughout their treatment and encouraged to make plans for their future despite their illness. This is done through workshops offering counseling, health education, and by working on their bodies and their self-esteem. Made up of psychologists, nurses, and social workers working in partnership with hospitals, Dessine-moi un mouton seeks to improve the quality of personal and family life for young people affected by disease.

www.dessinemoiunmouton.org

**THIS PAGE** Whether they dream of stroking an animal or becoming a knight, for these children, the essential is to see their dreams to reality.

## YOUTH FOUNDATION

Saint-Exupéry may no longer be with us, but his humanist ideas and view of the world turned toward others remain. In 2008, the Antoine de Saint-Exupéry Youth Foundation (FASEJ), founded by the writer's family and fans from aeronautical and literary backgrounds, launched a charitable initiative that would have stirred the enthusiasm of *The Little Prince*'s author: working to improve the lives of today's young people and prepare them for the future. Fully aware of the challenges faced by many young people who have all too often grown up in difficult environments, the foundation seeks to help them establish themselves as mature, responsible, and committed citizens. It relies on a vast international charity network, active in nearly 30 countries around the world, to carry out projects such as fighting against illiteracy and exclusion, building libraries, and helping people find employment. The impact that these initiatives have had in the world carries the echo of "Saint-Ex's" words in *The Wisdom of the Sands*: "Your task is not to foresee the future, but to enable it."

## LES AILES DU PETIT PRINCE

Les Ailes du Petit Prince (Wings of the Little Prince) is a non-profit association affiliated with the Antoine de Saint-Exupéry Youth Foundation. While the little prince may never have climbed aboard his friend the aviator's plane, this organization gives young people with disabilities the chance to meet pilots, discover the universe of aviation and aeronautics, and to take wing on an unforgettable maiden flight. Since 1998, thanks to a team of around 50 active members from the world of aviation and professionals who work with disabled children, the organization has afforded some 1,000 children between 7 and 14 years old (the same age we estimate Saint-Exupéry's protagonist to be) the opportunity to realize their dreams and experience a sense of freedom in spite of their disability.

www.lesailesdupetitprince.fr

# le petit monde

*" créé pour L'Enfant Et sa Santé "*

## LE PETIT MONDE

Le Petit Monde (Small World) is an association set up by Professor Pierre Chatelain in Lyon, France in 1997. Through its projects, the association aims to improve the quality of life of sick and/or hospitalized children. La Maison du Petit Monde was built on the site of the Mother and Children's Hospital in Lyon, making it possible for families to stay close to their child as they support them through their treatment.

This warm and friendly place has 54 rooms. It offers families the chance to recharge their batteries and mix with other families in the communal spaces.

The association has also created a game to prepare children for MRI scans in a light-hearted and reassuring way. The aim is, wherever possible, to remove the need for a child to be placed under general anesthetic. The scheme is currently employed in 10 hospitals across Europe.

www.lepetitmonde.com

**LEFT** Children forget their disability when they earn their wings on their first flight, thanks to Les Ailes du Petit Prince.

## LE PETIT PRINCE

Created in 1985, the Association Le Petit Prince hosts children and teenagers during school vacations with educational getaways and field classes on subjects ranging from the environment to new educational methods, focusing on encouraging community values such as self-respect and respect of others, tolerance of different views, co-operation, and re-channeling anger. Studies on relational harmony and humanism are offered through seminars as well as intergenerational stays, uniting people of all ages and promoting a better way of living together, collective intelligence, education, and peace.

Saint-Exupéry's tale resounds within the association's program. Not only is *The Little Prince* the intergenerational reference point, but its eponymous protagonist made new friends that he was forced to "tame" before he could become responsible for them...

www.lepetitprinceeasso.fr

## THE LITTLE PRINCE'S STARS

This Russian association, founded in 2007 and headed by Igor Shamraev with the support of the Saint-Exupéry Estate, seeks to put Antoine de Saint-Exupéry's philosophy into practice and help children in difficulty. It runs ecological projects, such as a communication campaign in partnership with Greenpeace which aims to draw attention to the risks of the use of chlorine in paper manufacturing. It has also organized a book swap in which hundreds of copies of *The Little Prince* travelled all around Russia, being passed from hand to hand.

www.lepetitprince.ru

# Conclusion

"Saint-Exupéry took hold of people and places with a smile. He swiftly made close and unexpected ties with everyone he met," wrote Léon Werth of his friend Antoine. Likewise, the little prince has the ability to strike up a friendship with everyone he meets, whether they are reading him for the first time or rediscovering him years later.

For this character is much more that the protagonist of a wonderful story. He is a travelling companion, a friend for life, a valuable and faithful supporter whom we keep at our sides throughout our existence. It is hardly an accident that he gives his name to hospitals and charitable organizations, that he is associated with the fight for children's rights, that he was chosen as a global symbol of the United Nations: he embodies the values of tolerance, education, respect for nature, broadening horizons, and caring for others.

The little prince hasn't aged a day since he was born. His svelte silhouette remains unchanged, as do his face and his round eyes, just as the face of Saint-Exupéry stays fixed for eternity in the photographs he has left us. The little prince cannot grow old; he is the same age as his readers. In him, we rediscover our childhood selves, adolescents and adults alike. Besides, we still don't know if *The Little Prince* is a book for children that can be read by grown-ups or if it's a story for adults that might be discovered by children. But that is of no importance. The essential thing is that it continues to enchant us and resonate with our deepest yearnings.

Perhaps one day he will come back. Saint-Exupéry himself maintained the mystery. "Send me word that he has come back..." reads the final page of the tale. But has the little prince really left? The reader knows that he is always there, hidden in the folds of their imagination, sheltered in the memory of the story that ensures he will live on forever. Simply open the book and you will see him again and hear him whisper softly in your ear: "If you please—draw me a sheep!"

# Bibliography

**La Mémoire du Petit Prince**
Jean-Pierre Guéno
& Jérôme Pecnard
(Éditions Jacob-Duvernet)

**Le Petit Prince, L'Œuvre**
(texts by Delphine Lacroix
and Virgil Tanase,
unavailable for purchase)

**Il était une fois... Le Petit Prince**
(texts collected and introduced
by Alban Cerisier,
Éditions Gallimard, coll. Folio)

**La Belle Histoire du Petit Prince**
d'Antoine de Saint Exupéry
(texts collected by Alban Cerisier
and Delphine Lacroix,
Éditions Gallimard)

**Antoine de Saint-Exupéry, dessins,
aquarelles, pastels, plumes et crayons**
(catalog introduced and created
by Delphine Lacroix and Alban
Cerisier, Éditions Gallimard)

**Saint-Exupéry**
Virgil Tanase (Éditions Gallimard,
coll. Folio Biographies)

**Saint Exupéry, L'archange et l'écrivain**
Nathalie des Vallières (Éditions
Gallimard, coll. Découvertes)

**Le Petit Prince, 60 ans après...
La véritable histoire**
(Special issue of "Lire"
monthly, 2006)

**Saint Exupéry, le héros éternel**
(Special issue
of "Le Point" weekly, 2014)

**Lettres à l'inconnue**
Antoine de Saint-Exupéry,
Éditions Gallimard

**La Véritable histoire du Petit Prince**
Alain Vircondelet,
Éditions Flammarion

# *Image Credits*